Elspeth
and
The Blue
Belle

Book One: Staying
Afloat

Claire Kelly

For Phillip, Olivia and George

Copyright @ 2023 Claire Kelly

Table of Contents

Chapter 1: Sums

Elspeth stepped lightly out of her flat into the mild, inviting, spring evening. Inhaling the scent of the hyacinths that she had planted in the little pot by her front door, she felt a sense of warm anticipation at the thought of the evening ahead. There were the brownies she had baked that afternoon which she would enjoy with her friends, and Minnie and Ava were always *interesting* company, to say the least. Plus there was the exciting news that she couldn't wait to share. She hadn't told anyone else yet; not even her mother.

Clutching the box of home-made brownies as she made the short trip around the corner to Minnie's flat, Elspeth reflected that she was glad she had friends who would appreciate her baking efforts. Peter wasn't a fan; in his eyes, the sugar to pleasure ratio simply didn't add up. Plus, as he was always quick to point out to Elspeth, baking things herself was *actually* rather a waste of time and money. "When you think about it," he had said, running his customary cost-time analysis, "by the time you've factored in the hour of your time that it's taken you to make them, plus the cost of buying all of the ingredients separately and the price of the energy taken to pre-heat the oven and then to actually *cook* them, it has probably cost you at least ten pounds. You could have utilised that time to do some hourly paid work – even at minimum wage that would be *over* ten pounds. And of course you could have just bought a box of brownies for half the price."

Elspeth tended to let these sorts of observations wash over her these days; when she had first started dating Peter three years ago, she had listened to him as one might a sage. Elspeth's own rather disastrous decisions in her early twenties had left her in debt and with little to show for her attempts to make a living as a sculptural artist, so Peter, a successful accountant with a healthy bank balance and a sensible attitude to quite literally *everything*, had seemed a shining model of how to live an adult life. Yet Elspeth had begun to see that Peter's approach left something vital out of the equation for contentment. Well, vital to her, at least. In baking the brownies, Elspeth found *joy*: joy in the velvety consistency of the rich mixture; joy in the warm, comforting aroma as they baked in the oven; joy in the first bite of a warm homemade brownie, perhaps enjoyed with a spoonful of smooth vanilla ice-cream. She knew that Peter wouldn't understand that, but she reasoned that everyone was different. That was part of the reason that they made such a good couple, she reflected; they brought very different things to their relationship.

Minnie opened the door, sporting a comfy pair of pyjamas, her dark, curly hair in disarray. Elspeth would have expected nothing more ... or less. The girls had known each other for years, and there was a tacit understanding that a night in at one of their flats would be a chance to relax and unwind. Elspeth herself was wearing comfy leggings and a sweatshirt.

"You brought brownies! Amazing. I love that you like baking. All that stuff's a mystery to me," said Minnie, ushering Elspeth in. "Ava's here already."

Elspeth went to greet Ava, who was demurely seated on the sofa with a fluffy cushion on her lap. Of her two best friends, Ava was perhaps the slightly less chaotic one, but she still had her moments. Elspeth got comfortable on the sofa next to her while Minnie disappeared to her tiny kitchen to make them some hot drinks and plate up the brownies.

Elspeth waited until Minnie was back and they had caught up on the events of each other's days before building up to her big reveal. "So," she said, smiling conspiratorially and leaning forward for maximum effect. "I have some news. *Big* news."

Ava and Minnie exchanged glances, clearly intrigued. "Go on!" said Ava. "What is it?"

"Last week," Elspeth paused for suspense, "Peter proposed!"

Elspeth waited for her friends' gasps of delight, congratulatory hugs and general excitement. She wasn't prepared for the several seconds of tumbleweed that followed her announcement.

"Oh." Ava said flatly. "That's ... um ... I didn't realise that you and Peter were at that stage, Elspeth."

Minnie nodded. "If anything, I thought you might split up soon," she offered insensitively.

"Split up? Why?" asked Elspeth incredulously, looking from one to the other. "I thought you'd be happy for me."

"We *are*," said Ava unconvincingly. "It's just ... well, you and Peter are very different. Which isn't necessarily a *bad* thing, but ... I guess that I've never felt your relationship really adds up."

"I just don't like him. That's all I'm saying," Minnie pronounced, curling her pyjama clad legs underneath her on the sofa and helping herself to another brownie.

"That's really not a supportive thing to say, Minnie," hissed Ava, sipping her drink. "I mean, you've got a point, obviously; Peter really *is* awful; but we should be nice about him for Elspeth's sake."

"I *am* here," Elspeth interjected. "Seriously, you two! I've never said anything negative about your boyfriends; even the *really* bad ones."

"You said Ewan smelled of pickles," pointed out Ava.

"True, but I didn't *necessarily* mean it as a criticism –"

"And you said Jake had the personality of raw dough," Minnie chimed in. "*Cloying* and *unpalatable*; I think those were the words you used to describe him. I mean, you were right, but –"

"Fair point," admitted Elspeth. It had been an uncharacteristically unkind comment made after a rather challenging camping weekend with Minnie and her now-ex, Jake. "*But*," Elspeth continued, "whenever I've said anything about *your* boyfriends, it's been for a *reason*, at least. That's the difference. Give me one good reason that you don't like Peter."

Ava screwed up her face in concentration. "He's … he's very interested in accounting. It's boring."

"Well, he's an accountant! Of course he's interested in accounting! It's his *job* to be interested in accounting! Not good enough. Try again."

Minnie and Ava were both silent for a moment. "I can't put my finger on it …" murmured Minnie. "He reminds me of someone – or some*thing*. It's to do with the way he stands." Minnie stood up and planted her feet so that the heels were almost together with the toes pointing slightly outwards. "Like this." She did a little demonstration walk across the floor. "And the way his brow always looks quite heavy, as if he's disapproving of something. And that dark blazer with the big shoulders he always wears for work." She opened her eyes wide with realisation. "I've got it!"

"Go on …"

"He reminds me of a *penguin*!"

Elspeth waited for clarification on why this was a point against Peter, while Ava nodded enthusiastically. "Yes! You're right, Minnie! I didn't know what it was until you said it, but that's totally it! And not one of the cute, fluffy penguins. One of the tall, *serious*, grumpy looking penguins. Like you've displeased them in some way and they're going to sigh loudly or tell you off."

Now it was Minnie's turn to nod enthusiastically. They, at least, were on the same page with this.

Elspeth raised her eyebrows. "And what's wrong with penguins?"

"Oh, nothing's wrong with penguins!" enthused Ava. "I love penguins. Just not, you know, a penguin-person. And definitely not a penguin-fiancée."

"Right. Thanks for that. I'm super-clear now about why you're not keen on Peter and I suppose I'll just have to call off the engagement because my fiancée reminds you both of a penguin and for some reason this is a problem."

Minnie nodded sympathetically. "Sorry, Elspeth. There'll be other men."

Elspeth looked at Minnie in disbelief. Her earlier pleasurable anticipation at sharing her news with Minnie and Ava had now utterly evaporated, and she began to wonder whether she needed to find some new friends. "No," she said slowly. "I'm not serious, Minnie. I'm not dumping Peter because he reminds me – I mean *you* – of a penguin. That would clearly be ridiculous."

"*Okay*," said Minnie with a shrug, giving Ava a despairing look as if to say: *You can't say we didn't tell her.*

There was a moment of awkward silence. "Well, in that case," Ava offered in a tone of forced jollity,

"I guess ... congratulations on your engagement, Elspeth!"

The girls clinked their mugs. "To Elspeth and Peter Pen- " Minnie stopped herself just in time. "To Elspeth and Peter!"

As Elspeth walked back to her flat later that evening, she couldn't help but be more than a little deflated by her friends' reactions to her news. Yes, she knew they had never been *particularly* keen on Peter, but that was nothing unusual. She, Minnie and Ava all had very different taste in men, which for the most part was a good thing: it meant that, in all the years of their friendship since meeting at sixth form college, there had never been a falling out over a man. Yet she hadn't anticipated that they would see the engagement as a *bad* thing; she'd assumed that, while Peter wasn't necessarily either of their type, they didn't actually *dislike* him. Clearly she had been wrong. And the trouble was, now that Minnie had said it, Elspeth could see exactly what she meant; Peter *did* have a grumpy penguin vibe about him. Elspeth shook her head. No, she mustn't let herself think like that. She and Peter were a great couple. They'd been dating for three years and he was a good influence on her. Unlike Elspeth, who had found it difficult to settle on a steady path since leaving University, Peter was a sensible, stable character. He was doing well at his accountancy firm and had helped to keep Elspeth on track with her goal of training, then working, as a paralegal. Elspeth appreciated his pragmatic, realistic perspective; it helped to stop her from pursuing her previously somewhat flighty ideas.

Yes, there were things about Peter that weren't *exactly* what Elspeth had imagined in a future husband. She had always been a bit of a romantic, but Peter had explained the fanciful nature of this and been very practical about it. Of course he was right: Valentine's Day *was* just a marketing ploy by card and gift companies to make people spend their money, so obviously he wasn't going to be conned into that. *No*, he had patiently explained to a disappointed Elspeth on their first Valentine's Day together, he would *not* be getting her a card and quite frankly he was surprised that she bought into all that nonsense. Of course, he was right, but it just ... might have been nice if he had. Then there was the actual proposal itself. Elspeth hadn't wanted anything particularly extravagant; she had always known that Peter wouldn't be a top of the Eiffel Tower type, but the proposal had felt a little ... flat. Peter had proposed over their Friday evening sausages and mash (her old takeaway habit from when she lived on her own had needed to be kerbed when they moved in together. As Peter had pointed out, the mark-up on the food was extortionate). At their simple kitchen table, lit by a pretty candle Elspeth had bought, Peter had asked Elspeth whether she would do him the honour of being his wife. His language choices were just right in Elspeth's mind: traditional and respectful. The less romantic part was when Elspeth held her hand out expectantly for a ring, only to see Peter looking at her in surprise.

"Oh. You weren't expecting a ring *now*, were you?"

"Um ... I just thought that was how people did it, you know?"

"Well, *illogical* people, maybe!" Peter had chuckled. "What would be the point in me spending money on a ring without knowing your size or what type you like? Once I have that information then I can find the best value one and get it all done in one trip to a shop, you see?"

"Yes … I suppose that makes sense," Elspeth had muttered, bristling slightly at the implications of the phrase *get it all done*, as if buying her an engagement ring were somehow a chore. Always keen to see the positives though, she had then brightened at the thought. "And it'll be romantic, won't it? Going shopping together to look at engagement rings? You can show me what you would like too!"

"Oh, I've already chosen mine," Peter said helpfully. "It's in the sale. That's part of the reason I proposed tonight – I thought now would be the best time to do it before it's back on at full price again."

Elspeth had nodded. Of course, it made perfect sense. Why spend unnecessary money on a ring and do multiple trips to the jewellers just for the sake of a moment? Peter was, as usual, *technically* right.

They had finished their sausages and mash happily enough together, both excited in different ways by the new fact of their engagement. Elspeth couldn't wait to tell her friends (well, look how *that* had turned out, she reflected as she rounded the corner to their flat) and Peter was delighted about them formalising their relationship. He had recently read an article that estimated the additional cost of living as a single person was *£860 per month* once you factored in rent, bills and general household expenses. Provided they had a modest wedding, a partnership would be a real money saver for them both over the long term.

Letting herself into their one-bedroom, ground floor flat, Elspeth smiled as she opened the door and stepped into the hallway. They had their own front door, a real luxury compared to Elspeth's previous house-share rooms and the tiny studio flat she had rented as a single person. Elspeth had made the flat as homely as she could. The landlord had agreed to let her decorate a couple of the rooms when they moved in, provided that she ran the colour choices by him. She had opted for a delicate shade of blue in the hallway, which looked at once pretty and stylish. The living room was a calming sage green: her sanctuary. Peter hadn't been keen on redecorating: why put your own time and money into improving someone else's property? There was nothing to be gained from it, in his opinion. But for Elspeth, to have a space of her own that she could design in a way that made her happy was a privilege. She had bought the paints and roller trays with her own money (she and Peter had separate accounts) and had completed all of the decorating single-handedly with a little help from a neighbour's step-ladder. She knew that it would be some years before she and Peter could buy a place of their own. Peter said that interest rates looked to be more favourable in a few years' time – now *really* wasn't the time to take on a significant mortgage debt - and they could save up more for a deposit in the meantime. They had been living in the rented flat for around eight months now. Elspeth made a mental note to check the terms of the tenancy to make sure they could renew the lease for another year.

Peter was on the sofa in the living room watching a documentary when Elspeth arrived home. He loved documentaries. Elspeth wasn't so keen, but felt that she probably should better herself and so was trying to get interested in them too. Sitting down next to Peter, Elspeth leaned in to him slightly to snuggle up.

"Sorry," Peter mumbled, moving to the right. "I'll give you some room."

"No, I didn't mean that. I was … never mind. How was work?"

"Oh, same old, you know. Lots of meetings this afternoon so I didn't get much done."

"And how's that new girl working out?"

"New girl?"

"You know, the one that you're supervising. Maria, isn't it?"

"Maria? Um … I can't remember."

"What do you mean, you can't remember?" laughed Elspeth, playfully nudging Peter's arm. "You were talking about her last week. How she's come in with all of these ideas for the firm but she doesn't have the experience to understand what will work. You know!"

"Oh, *her*. Well, I don't really come into contact with her much, so …"

Elspeth frowned. There were only four people in Peter's team and he was supervising Maria. She decided to drop it; maybe there were work politics at play that he didn't want to talk about.

She tried again to snuggle up to him, and this time he didn't move away. In fairness, he was already right at the edge of the sofa so he didn't have much choice. Elspeth's mind drifted as she semi-watched the documentary while privately reflecting on her situation: she was twenty-eight, she was a paralegal and she was engaged. Considering her prospects five years ago (she shuddered at the memory) things were far more positive now than she had thought they might be. Back then, struggling to find a path for herself with her Art degree, she had spent years trying, unsuccessfully, to make a living through her art. Her work – mostly large sculptural pieces in wood and metalwork - was *good*, but, she had to admit, it just wasn't *the best*. And to make a living in that world, you had to be the best *and* to have a certain amount of opportunity come your way. It had just never happened for Elspeth. She had sold several of her pieces, mostly at a loss when she considered the time and materials taken to produce them, and had a portfolio of sketches and photographs of them stored away at the back of her wardrobe. She almost couldn't look at the portfolio now. Rather than representing possibility and talent, she looked at it and saw failure.

Her enthusiastic pursuit of an art career had led her into debt: she had even tried putting on her own exhibition to raise her profile, but the sales of a few pieces had nowhere near covered the cost of staging the event. She had made a shortfall every month and her credit card debt had slowly mounted. It was when she met Peter three years ago that her life changed direction. Utterly practical, he had immediately pronounced her art career unviable and had advised her to take steps to pursue something more concrete. Training, then eventually working as a paralegal had been game changing for Elspeth's finances. Her debt was now shrinking and she had enough to pay her share of the rent every month. Peter insisted that they pay half each of everything despite him earning significantly more than her; he explained it was important that she take responsibility for herself. And there was no way he would open a joint account with Elspeth for the bills and rent: he had carefully guarded his credit history and didn't want to take any risks. She understood. She knew that she had been something of a liability.

And now here she was: engaged to Peter, living in their homely shared flat and able to support herself financially. She glanced surreptitiously at Peter as they sat on the sofa together. She knew what Minnie and Ava *meant*, but she had her reasons for accepting Peter's proposal. He might not be the most exciting man in the world and there *was* something somewhat serious and disapproving in his demeanour at times, but Elspeth thought that maybe that was what she needed.

Chapter 2: Not the One

Elspeth had mixed feelings about telling her mother of her engagement. On the one hand, she thought Janice would probably be happy about the situation, but you could never tell with Janice. Elspeth guessed Janice had mixed feelings on Peter: on the one hand she wouldn't have chosen him for herself (as she told Elspeth, she was attracted to powerful men with charisma), yet Janice *did* seem to see Peter as something of a success, what with his good education and steady job. It remained to be seen how Janice would react to him as a future son-in-law.

They were due to meet that Saturday morning for tea and cake in a local café. Having returned to her native town after three years away at University then four in London trying unsuccessfully to 'make it' in the art world, Elspeth told herself that she was fortunate to live close enough to her mother for them to be part of each other's lives. She told herself this quite regularly, yet somehow she *still* hadn't managed to convince herself; Janice wasn't the easiest of women. Elspeth took a deep breath before entering the pretty café, with its shabby chic interior and comforting aroma of freshly baked cakes. Janice was already there, had clearly ordered coffee and cake for herself and was already complaining to the server. Elspeth ordered a pot of tea and a lemon slice at the counter, before arriving at Janice's table in time to catch the gist of it.

"It's very claggy," Janice was saying to the server. "You know, heavy and sticky."

"Oh, I'm so sorry!" The girl was new at the café and, unlike the other members of staff, didn't realise that the best way to approach Janice was not to approach her at all. "It's quite a heavy fruit cake. I thought it was supposed to be like that. Would you like something different? I could take that away." The girl reached her hand out for the plate, but Janice quickly swiped it out of her reach.

"No sense wasting this now, is there?" she said accusingly. "No, I might as well see if I can get through it, but I'll have a scone with cream and jam as well to make up for it. On the house, of course."

"Of course," agreed the server, scurrying back to the kitchen.

Elspeth resignedly took a seat opposite Janice. "Really? You couldn't just eat the cake without causing a fuss?"

"Claggy."

"Hmm. Anyway, I have some news, mum." Elspeth paused for effect. "Last week … Peter proposed!"

Elspeth wasn't sure exactly what she had been expecting, but Janice's response took her a little off guard. "Oh, did he? Well that's nice of him, I suppose. Is he sure?"

"What do you mean, *nice of him*? *Is he sure*? Of course he's sure! And he *wants* to marry me, obviously. Why on earth would you say it's *nice* of him?"

Janice slowly sipped her coffee, utterly unruffled by Elspeth evidently having taken offence. "Well, he's got prospects, hasn't he? And he's a sensible type of chap. Wouldn't be for me, of course – *far* too dull – but that's not a problem for you, I suppose. No, I just thought he'd marry someone more his own … intellectual level."

Elspeth's tea and cake had arrived during Janice's pronouncements, brought by the same girl who had served Janice and was visibly terrified to approach their table. Elspeth bit into her lemon slice aggressively, pausing for just a moment to savour its bitter sweetness before returning her attention back to her mother.

"Are you suggesting that I'm not *clever enough* for Peter?"

Janice shrugged. "Your words, not mine, Elspeth."

Elspeth found herself trapped in the strange, twisting web of words that she always got into with her mother. "No, *you* implied it. I was just clarifying."

Janice made a face, clearly bored with the conversation. "I've got some news too," she said, abruptly changing the subject back to herself. "Me and Margot have booked a cruise for next summer. I'm going to need to buy some new shoes. Probably red ones to go with that long dress I've got; you know, the one that shows off my cleavage. And Margot says we should definitely dress up in the evenings because there are lots of wealthy old men on these cruises …"

As Janice droned on about the upcoming cruise and her and Margot's outfit choices while happily polishing off her 'claggy' cake plus the additional free scone, Elspeth couldn't help but feel a little disheartened at her mother's reaction to her engagement. She had known that it wouldn't be all smiles and congratulations, but she had expected a bit more interest than this. Janice hadn't even asked to see her engagement ring – not that there actually *was* one to see yet, Elspeth reminded herself. She was hoping that she and Peter could go engagement ring shopping that weekend; she had suggested it twice already but received a lukewarm response. She resolved to raise it again with Peter that evening and try to get him to commit.

Peter didn't commit to going engagement ring shopping that week. Or the week after that. Elspeth began to feel that she was pestering him and, aware that she didn't want to turn into some sort of haranguing fiancée, she let the matter drop for the moment. It was the third week after the engagement that she began to suspect that Peter's reluctance was down to more than being busy. He seemed to have gone off the idea of the engagement entirely. Whenever she tried to raise it, perhaps to talk about *when* they might get married or *where* they might hold the wedding or *who* they would invite, Peter would look uncomfortable, slipping into an exaggerated penguin-stance (Elspeth had to admit that Minnie really did have a point) and dismissing her questions with an irritated frown. The more that she tried to talk to him, the more he seemed to pull away.

It was the Thursday evening of the following week and Elspeth was on her way home from a pizza and prosecco evening with Minnie. It had been a warm day and she was attempting a chic summer look she had seen in a magazine: a plain white floaty maxi-dress and delicate gold sandals. It had been a beautifully comfortable outfit for the day, but a few minutes after she left Minnie's flat, the weather broke and the heavens opened. Elspeth was drenched in moments, the previously floaty white material now sticking to her uncomfortably. Trudging along in her now squelching sandals, Elspeth gasped as a car drove through a puddle in the gutter next to her, splattering her with muddy water. Elspeth stopped in her tracks, the rain falling around her and soaking her hair as she looked aghast at her pretty dress, now covered in splatters of brown. She had reached the main street in town, and realised she was bathed in the welcoming glow from the floor-to-ceiling windows of the swanky new wine bar. Elspeth looked into the window to surreptitiously check her reflection, and as she did so she saw beyond into the sophisticated, inviting interior. Time slowed as she took in the scene before her: Peter and a young woman, sitting on high stools at a small table for two, each with what looked like a Cosmopolitan cocktail. Peter never drank Cosmopolitans. Peter wasn't *fun* enough to drink Cosmopolitans; he objected to the high mark-up on alcohol in bars at the best of times, let alone for a tiny, sugary drink like that. Elspeth rubbed her eyes in case she wasn't seeing things clearly; perhaps it was just a man who *looked like* Peter. But no, there was his briefcase propped neatly against the leg of his chair, and that was the smart grey and white striped tie Elspeth had bought him last Christmas. *Maybe it's just a work drink*, she said to herself, shivering in the rain and quickly assessing the woman Peter was with. She certainly looked like a work colleague. She was wearing a black skirt and blazer and Elspeth noted the second briefcase propped against the foot of her chair. Elspeth gave a sigh of relief. Just work colleagues. She was about to turn up the street to go home and get out of the rain, when she saw a movement out of the corner of her eye which made her turn her gaze back to the couple. The woman had reached out to touch Peter's hand across the table. They were both smiling in a way that Elspeth immediately realised was not simply friendly. As she watched, unconsciously holding her breath, Peter reached out and brushed a stray lock of the

21

woman's dark hair away from her face. It was a gesture of intimacy. Elspeth felt sick.

This was Maria. There was no doubt in Elspeth's mind. Maria had been conspicuous in her absence from Peter's accounts of his work days over the last few weeks. There was plenty of talk of Ted, of Seema and of Katie, the other members of his small team, but he never mentioned Maria despite Elspeth knowing that he was supervising her. Well, so *that* was what was going on. Elspeth toyed with her options: go home and cry on the sofa then challenge Peter when he eventually arrived back? Or march into the wine bar *right now*, her mascara running down her cheeks, her long blonde hair dripping wet and her white, mud-spattered dress clinging to her? Elspeth knew that she must look like some sort of jilted bride from a gothic novel, but she had to go and confront him – with *her*.

Pushing open the door to the wine bar, Elspeth was met by a sophisticated fragrance, the delicate clinking of glasses, and the murmur of intimate conversations. Ignoring the puddle of water she had left behind her on entering, she made her squelchy way across the bar to Peter's table. She said nothing as she stood there for a few moments, waiting until Peter noticed her. When he did, his expression was priceless: absolute horror. His eyes widened and his mouth opened as he stared at a dripping, seething Elspeth. He muttered something incoherent, and Maria turned to see what he was staring at. Clearly surprised to see the dishevelled figure of Elspeth standing silently but purposefully next to their table in her long, white dress, she raised her eyebrows quizzically at Peter.

"Do you, um, know this lady, Peter?"

Peter was uncharacteristically at a loss for words. His mouth still open, he nodded slowly, unable to take his eyes off the terrible spectacle of his fiancée.

"He's *supposed* to be *marrying* me," said Elspeth, her voice threatening and an octave lower than her usual bright tone.

"What, *now*?" asked Maria, clearly mistaking Elspeth's attempt at floaty white summer chic for some sort of bridal gown.

"Would you like to explain yourself, Peter?" asked Elspeth. "I'm sure Maria would like to know that you're engaged to *me*, and I would certainly like to know why you're having an intimate drink with *her*."

"You're *engaged*? Peter, you never told me that! You said it was just a case of waiting until the lease ran out and then you'd end things!"

This was worse than Elspeth had imagined. She glared at Peter, her eyes flashing, now fully channelling her Miss-Havisham-like demeanour. "You told her you were planning to end things with me *when the lease ran out*? You only proposed to me three weeks ago! What on earth are you playing at, Peter?"

Peter put his head in his hands. By now their table had attracted the attention of the other staff and customers in the wine bar, who were waiting intently for Peter's explanation.

"I ... I'm sorry, Elspeth," he managed. "It just ... happened."

Elspeth stared at him in disbelief. "But *how* did it happen, Peter? How do you tell one woman you want to get engaged to her while telling another woman that you're about to end that relationship? I just don't understand."

Peter shrugged and spread his hands. "It was in the sale," he said desperately.

Elspeth looked at him uncomprehendingly. "What do you mean? What was in the sale?"

"The engagement ring that *I* wanted. I just thought it looked like such a bargain I should get it straight away. So I bought it. I didn't tell you that at the time. It's been hidden in my bedside drawer. Then I thought we'd better get engaged so I could wear it, so I proposed to you. I didn't think that things with Maria would take off the way that they have." Peter broke off to smile shyly at Maria, and Elspeth was struck by how utterly un-penguin-like he looked in that moment. He never smiled like that with Elspeth. "And then, when I realised that maybe I wanted to be with Maria instead, I thought there was no point in telling you before the lease on our flat ran out – we've got to pay until the end of the twelve months anyway and there's no sense in spending money unnecessarily. It just … all went a bit too far."

Elspeth couldn't believe what she was hearing. "So, just to be clear Peter, you proposed to me because you had bought *yourself* an engagement ring and you wanted a reason to keep it, then you decided to keep up the charade of being engaged to me so you didn't lose any rent money. Is that what you're saying?"

There were murmurs from the adjacent tables and much disapproving shaking of heads.

"What an *idiot*," someone muttered.

"You're better off without him, love," came the sage advice from another table.

Elspeth glanced at Maria, expecting to see *her* disgust at Peter's behaviour. Instead, Maria was nodding. She reached over and touched Peter's hand across the table. "Rent is *really* expensive," she said earnestly. "It's the biggest line in most people's budgets. It's important to take it into consideration."

"Wow." Elspeth had a strange sensation, as if she were waking up from a dream and seeing herself from an outside perspective. Here she was, a creative, kind, loving person, and she had been prepared to accept *this*. She understood that Peter wasn't malicious in any way, he was just sensible to the point of emotional ineptitude. And now he had found somebody who was the same. Somebody who understood the way he saw the world because she saw it that way too. They would be perfect for each other. Elspeth let out a long, cathartic breath, exhaling all of the tension, resentment and hurt. "Thank you, Peter, for helping me to come to my senses," she said. "You're dumped. Obviously. I hope you two will be very happy together. I expect you to sleep on the sofa tonight, to move out tomorrow and to pay your share of the rent until the end of our lease." Elspeth turned to the attentive faces in the wine bar. 'Does that sound reasonable?" she asked.

"More than reasonable!" one man shouted.

"I'd throw 'im out tonight!" offered a woman.

"He needs a kick in the – " An elderly lady was mercifully cut off by the general muttering in support of Elspeth.

Elspeth gathered her dripping skirts, tilted her chin upwards and made an *almost* dignified exit from the wine bar. The rain had stopped and the earth smelt fresh. *Petrichor*, Elspeth thought to herself, remembering the Ancient Greek word for the beautiful smell that followed rain after a dry spell. There was a sense of release, of cleansing. Elspeth knew that, no matter how hard this might feel now, splitting up with Peter was absolutely the best thing for her. He was not the one. Perhaps there wasn't a one. But, she reflected as she let herself into their pretty flat, there would certainly be better ones than *that*.

Chapter 3: A Better Fit

Arriving home, drenched and emotionally depleted, Elspeth ran herself a bubble bath in which she immersed herself for over half an hour. Emerging from the steamy bathroom feeling warmed and comforted, she put on her favourite old pyjamas – the ones Peter hated – and settled herself in bed with a book to wait for Peter to come back and fetch his pyjamas and toothbrush before making up a bed on the sofa for himself. Yet despite Elspeth's reasonable offer, Peter didn't sleep on the sofa at their flat that night. He didn't come back that night at all. Falling asleep over her book after midnight, Elspeth tossed and turned all night, unable to fully relax and half expecting to hear his key in the door. When the dawn began to peep through the curtains at 4.30am, she tiptoed to the living room to confirm her suspicions: Peter hadn't slept at the flat. He must be with Maria.

Unable to get back to sleep, Elspeth got up groggily and padded to the kitchen to make herself a cup of tea and a bowl of cereal, feeling the weak rays of the early morning sun as they shone in through the front window of their ground floor flat. Everything would be different now, she realised. It wasn't that she hadn't experienced breakups and life-changes before; she'd had three fairly serious boyfriends prior to Peter, one of whom she had even lived with. Yet she realised that this time it *was* different. Sure as she was after the events of the previous evening that she was most definitely better off without Peter, Elspeth had spent the previous few months and even years imagining that Peter would be – well – her life-partner. She had spent the last few weeks imagining that he would be her husband. More than that, she realised, she had been *shaped* by Peter. Her previous boyfriends had all been free-spirits; in some ways that had been a contributing factor in the break ups. Artistic, creative types, none of them had wanted to settle down or to mould or advise Elspeth in any way, so when they went their own separate ways, she had still felt, more or less, that she was the same person she was when she met them. With Peter it was different. He had appeared in her life at a time when she *wanted* someone to help her to change; to be more responsible. And he had. In many ways, Elspeth was grateful to him for that. Yet, as she sipped her morning cup of tea, she reflected that she had only been this version of herself with Peter. How would this version of Elspeth function in the world without Peter? Could she even be this version of herself without him? Did she even want to?

Elspeth knew that she really wasn't in the right frame of mind to go to work that day, but also knew that any sort of undocumented absence was frowned upon. Her workplace had high expectations, especially from her no-nonsense boss, Nina. Elspeth had already had a few notices from HR about lateness and several warnings from Nina and the other partners about missing work deadlines. Gathering herself after another cup of sugary tea, she donned her smart work dress and drove the five miles to her office in her old Fiat Punto. As she drew up in the car park, she felt herself weighed down by the day ahead of her. In some ways, she was glad that she had re-trained as a paralegal: she earned a relatively decent wage and *some* of her colleagues were pleasant enough. Yet it also made her very aware of her age. Most of the other paralegals at the firm were in their early twenties, fresh from law degrees and doing the paralegal work for experience and as a stepping stone to a training contract. The work she did was at once taxing and monotonous: she needed to be thorough and meticulous so as not to miss things, but as the most junior member of the team she would also be the one doing the most tedious tasks. Today, and all month in fact, would be spent on document bundling. She thought back for a moment to the heady days of her art course at University, where she had specialised in working with wood and metalwork to design and create intricate contemporary sculptures. She had imagined then that her life would always be like that: creating, designing, working with her hands, using her skills. How different this was. Still, Elspeth reminded herself: she had bills to pay, and soon enough she would be paying them on her own. That was something she had yet to work out. With a sigh, she got out of her car and walked into the building.

Arriving at her work station, Elspeth groaned when she saw the pile of document boxes awaiting her. She knew that, what with her mind taken up with thoughts of her engagement for the last three weeks, she had not really been keeping up with her workload. Relatively inexperienced in this sector as she was, she *had* thought that perhaps some of her workload would be reallocated when it became clear to her superiors that she couldn't do it all during her nine to five working day. Apparently not. Yawning audibly, she settled down to the boxes of documents awaiting her attention.

At first Elspeth was confused by the tapping sensation on her arm. "Wha-?" she mumbled, resting her head back onto the pile of paperwork.

"Elspeth!" Nina's voice was shrill and firm. "You need to wake up!"

Elspeth came around with a start to see the faces of her colleagues staring at her in surprise. She sat up slowly in her office chair as she comprehended what had happened, before realising that she had a post-it note stuck to her cheek where she had been resting on it as she slept.

"Oh no, I'm so sorry," she murmured, slowly peeling the post-it note from her face. "I don't know what happened. I was looking through the files on the Brown and Williams case and –"

"And you fell asleep. *That's* what happened," Nina sharply interrupted.

"Yes, I'm sorry. I must have. I've had a difficult time, you see," Elspeth began to explain. "I split up with my boyfriend last night, and –"

"You're not the only one here with a personal life, Elspeth," snapped Nina. "The only difference is, the rest of us don't bring it into work with us. Now sort yourself out and come and see me in my office in half an hour."

Elspeth rolled her eyes. Unfortunately, she didn't wait quite long enough. Nina saw her. Boy, she was in trouble now.

Knocking on the door of Nina's office, having splashed water on her face in the toilets to wake herself up, Elspeth felt a degree of trepidation. Nina was known for being tough.

"Sit down." Nina gestured to a chair on the other side of her desk.

Elspeth took a seat. "I'm sorry about earlier," she began, "it's just that Peter, my boyfriend …"

She trailed off as she processed Nina's furious look. "I'm not interested, Elspeth. Not at all. Did you know that I'm a single mother to three children? No?

I didn't think so. Because I come here and do my job!" Elspeth paused to reflect on Nina's revelation. No, Elspeth *hadn't* realised Nina was a single mother with three children. Come to think of it, Elspeth had never thought of Nina as having a life outside of work *at all*. When Elspeth arrived in the morning, Nina would be in her office. When Elspeth left the office to take breaks and go for her lunch hour, Nina would be in her office. When Elspeth fled the building at five, Nina would be in her office. Always immaculately presented, always sharp as a tack, always efficient, Nina was the ultimate corporate professional. Elspeth looked at her through new eyes as Nina took a breath and opened the file in front of her. Elspeth's file. "Now, I assume you are aware that your probationary year with us is coming to an end in a month's time?"

"Is it? I hadn't realised. Shouldn't I have got an e-mail from HR or something?"

"You did," said Nina drily. "Two weeks ago. I know, because I was copied in. They asked you to make an appointment with me to review your progress. You didn't."

"Oh." Elspeth knew that she wasn't the best at keeping on top of her work e-mails. There were just so *many*. So sometimes she just … ignored them.

"So you're due for your review anyway," Nina continued. "Now's as good a time as any."

Nina took a review sheet from the front of Elspeth's folder. "So, I suppose we might as well go through the motions," said Nina. "What do you think has been going well during your probationary year?"

Go through the motions? Elspeth gulped. She hadn't expected this at all.

"Um, well, I think I've learned a lot this year about the key processes involved in legal work and I get on well with my colleagues."

"Right." Nina's gaze was severe. "And how do you feel that you have contributed to the team this year?"

"Well, I've been doing a lot of work with Casey on the Brown and Williams case, and –"

"About that," Nina interrupted. "Casey fed back that the team missed a filing deadline because you were late with the bundling."

"Well, *yes*, but the documents appeared on my desk on a Friday afternoon and the deadline was noon on the Monday, so ..."

"So?"

"So I didn't have time to get it done. I mean, Saturday and Sunday aren't working days."

"Elspeth," Nina said exasperatedly, "this is a *law firm*. Have you noticed that you're the first one to leave every day?"

Elspeth nodded. "Yes," she said slowly. "I have. But I thought people just ... wanted to stay."

Now that she said it aloud, she realised how ridiculous it sounded. Of course they didn't *want* to stay. They were staying to at least *try* to keep on top of their ridiculous workloads. Elspeth sat back in her chair. She suddenly saw her job from an entirely new perspective.

"So, I'm not doing well here, then?" she offered.

Nina looked at her incredulously. "No, Elspeth. You're not. I would have thought you would be well aware of this. HR have been in touch with you several times about lateness in the mornings, several of the partners have copied me in about missed deadlines and shoddy work and you spend most of your time chatting with colleagues in the kitchen. Did you honestly think this was going well?"

Did she? Now that Elspeth considered it, she realised that she hadn't really thought about it much at all. To her, this was just a job she had to do in order to pay her rent and reduce her debt. She had thought that, as long as she kept going, that was enough. How wrong she had been.

"I take it I haven't passed my probationary year, then?"

"No, Elspeth, you haven't." Nina uncharacteristically softened for a moment and Elspeth saw a glimpse of the person under the professional mask. "Look, I know it's hard. Working in a place like this is demanding. It requires sacrifice. You can't just do it as a nine-to-five and forget about it. But we get dozens of enquiries about paralegal roles every week, Elspeth. People see it as a way of getting a foot in the door. We can't keep people on who aren't pulling their weight. I'm sorry, Elspeth. Obviously you should work for the remaining term of your probationary contract while you look for something else. Something that's a better fit for you. And, just for the record, it sounds like your boyfriend wasn't that great. I heard you telling Sophia about him in the kitchen. You're probably better off without him."

As Elspeth returned to her desk, the piles of documents still awaiting her attention despite her knowing full well that her contract here would be ending in a few weeks, she reflected on Nina's words. *Something that's a better fit for you.* She knew that, on one level, Nina was absolutely right: this job *wasn't* the best fit for her. Elspeth found little satisfaction in it and, if she was absolutely honest, found it rather dull and knew that she didn't have the right attitude to it. The difficulty was, that the thing that Elspeth *did* enjoy and find satisfaction in - designing, creating and making sculptures – simply wasn't an economically viable option. Elspeth thought back to the pieces she had created over the years, at art school and beyond. She had excelled at intricate wood and metal work, so sculpture had become the most obvious medium for her. She had created beautiful pieces, often designed for outdoor exhibition: metalwork birds mounted on slender supports and seeming to soar into the air; tall, intricate, whirling ironwork obelisks stretching up towards the sky; beautifully carved, smooth wooden figures that added structure to a landscape. There had been a demand for her pieces, mostly as architectural additions for garden designs, but it simply hadn't been financially viable. A piece could take her weeks, sometimes over a month to complete from start to finish. Charging for the materials and for her time, even at a very modest rate, would mean she would need to charge hundreds or thousands of pounds for a sculpture in order to support herself. People liked her work, but not enough to pay that much for it. All of the pieces she had sold she had done so at a loss, once she factored in the time she had put in to create them.

Elspeth had known for a long time, even before she met Peter, that her art wasn't a sustainable career; she needed to do something else. She had thought perhaps paralegal work could be it. Now, she understood that this probably wasn't the right choice for her either. She could apply for other jobs at other firms, of course she could, but her heart just wasn't in it. And as Nina had made crystal clear, this wasn't a job that one could do half-heartedly. As with her relationship, Elspeth would need to go back to the drawing board.

Chapter 4: Triple-Whammy

It was a week after her meeting with Nina that Elspeth received a text from Peter, politely explaining that he would like to come to the flat one evening soon to collect his things. He had his own key, which he would keep until the tenancy ran out as he was still paying half of the rent money, so could let himself in if Elspeth was out. Tempted as she was to try to avoid him, Elspeth decided that it would be more helpful to speak to him face-to-face. In addition to giving her a degree of emotional closure, there were practical things they would need to sort out.

Peter arrived after work on Thursday evening, parking his smart, practical car on the road outside their flat. Elspeth went to the door to meet him. She knew that this meeting could be awkward; the last time she had seen or spoken to Peter was in the wine bar before her dramatic, soggy exit. Elspeth had resolved to approach things maturely and politely; she had enough challenges with her current work and financial situation to want more drama where Peter was concerned.

"Peter. Hi. Come in." She maintained a neutral tone as she opened the front door wide and stood back to allow him into the pretty hallway that she had painted. "Would you like a cup of tea before you get started on your things?"

Peter was evidently surprised – and relieved – at Elspeth's moderate, reasonable demeanour. "Yes please," he said cautiously. "That would be appreciated."

They went into the kitchen and Elspeth took a mug from the cupboard, suddenly realising the extent of how unpleasant the next hour or so would feel. The mug she was holding was Peter's. Of course, he would want to take it with him. And, now that she came to think about it, the kettle was Peter's. And the toaster. And the microwave. She had somehow imagined that Peter would just be picking up his clothes and his personal items; she had forgotten that significantly more than half of the household items in the flat were his as well.

"Erm, I suppose you'll be wanting to take this one with you," she said, holding out the mug. "I could use one of mine for your tea so we don't have to wash this one, if you like."

"Good idea," said Peter. "I'm glad you're here while I do this actually, Elspeth. Me and Maria were talking and I'd like to take as many of my items as I can while I'm here. But I understand that I was in the wrong to mislead you as I did," he continued, clearly in what he imagined was a spirit of generosity, "so I wanted to make sure you are in agreement about what is mine. If there *is* disagreement about anything, I can come back again in a week when we have both had time to think about it and write down the reasons why we each think we should have claim to it."

Elspeth nodded glumly. "It's OK Peter. I understand that most of this is yours. I wouldn't try to take it. There's just one thing that I would appreciate you leaving for me."

"What's that?"

"The kettle. I think I'll need a nice cup of tea after you've left."

Peter nodded. "That's fine, Elspeth," he said. "Consider it my gift to you. By way of an apology for what happened."

Elspeth almost laughed out loud. As if a kettle could make up for the way he had treated her! Yet she understood that, in Peter's world, this was an attempt to make amends. After all, he had paid good money for that kettle. Even if, as she now remembered, he *had* bought it in the sale.

Peter disappeared up to the bedroom to begin packing his clothes, and Elspeth decided to watch a talent show in order to take her mind off the reality of their separation. That was one good thing about Peter moving out, she reflected; she didn't need to try to feign interest in any more documentaries. It took Peter around two hours to pack his things and load them into his car; he would need to do two trips to wherever it was he was taking his things. Elspeth didn't enquire as to where he was staying. She had a strong suspicion it would be with Maria, but knowing for sure would not have helped her state of mind, so she decided not to raise it. Peter popped into the sitting room to check a few items with Elspeth as he packed - it became clear that everything from the table lamps to the dinner plates to the toothbrush holder in the bathroom was Peter's. Elspeth would have to make do for a while. It was fortunate that they had been renting the flat furnished, so she would at least have a sofa to sit on and a bed to sleep in. Once the car was packed for his second trip, Peter joined Elspeth in the sitting room to say goodbye.

"So where will you live when the lease runs out here?" he asked.

"I'm not sure," Elspeth admitted. "I thought maybe I'd get a short extension here while I figure things out. When does it run out, anyway?"

Peter looked at her in surprise. "You mean you don't know? I assumed you'd have checked! It runs out a week on Friday."

"What? A week on Friday! Why didn't you tell me?" Elspeth exclaimed.

"Well, you knew it was coming up soon. You *are* an adult, Elspeth," Peter pointed out reasonably. "Obviously we haven't spoken since the ... incident at the wine bar, and I assumed that you would have given some thought to your situation. All of the documents regarding the flat are in the folder clearly labelled 'flat documents'. It's been sitting on the bookshelf right in front of you for the last week. I can't imagine why you wouldn't have had a look."

"Oh. I see." Elspeth was disheartened. "Well, I'll just contact the landlord in the morning and explain that I'll need a bit more time," she said. "I'm sure they'll understand."

"No, Elspeth, I doubt that will be a possibility. My understanding is that they have new tenants moving in two weeks on Monday. If you had wanted to extend the lease, you would have needed to do so weeks ago."

"So I'll be homeless?"

"Well, I don't think you need to be quite that dramatic about it. It's up to you what you do. You can find another place to rent. You are twenty-eight and working full-time, Elspeth. You can rent somewhere. Or you could stay with one of your friends. Or your mother."

Elspeth stared blankly at the wall. How had she let herself get into this mess? In hindsight, of course she *had known* that the lease was running out soon. It was just that she always relied on Peter to sort these things out. In a moment of clarity, Elspeth understood that she needed to grow up. She had made assumptions that Peter was somehow responsible for her. He wasn't. Elspeth had a sudden terrifying image of living with Janice for the rest of her life. She had to find an alternative.

The moment Peter had left, Elspeth began scouring property websites for rentals in her area. It was utterly dispiriting. Based on the fact that there were only a few weeks left on her probationary contract at work and she had no job security, Elspeth realised that most landlords would not even consider taking her on as a tenant. Even if she could find one who would, it appeared that a studio flat in the area would be too much for her to commit to long term now that she would be paying the rent on her own. Taking a deep breath, she searched for house-shares, before realising that no, as a twenty-eight year old she simply couldn't face going back to that again. She resolved to see if Minnie and Ava were free to meet up the next evening. They both had one-bedroom flats of their own; perhaps one of them would be able to help.

After a somewhat demotivating day going through box after box of documents at work and a meeting with HR where they asked her to fill out a form with the details of her departure from the law firm, Elspeth messaged Minnie and Ava, inviting them over for a curry so that they could talk about her impending housing disaster. She and Minnie had flat-shared once, back in their early twenties, and it hadn't gone *too* badly - if you discounted the accusations of food theft that Minnie had unreasonably levelled at Elspeth – so Elspeth was hopeful that there could be the offer of Minnie's sofa for a few weeks. Ava also might be in a position to help; her flat was a bit bigger than Minnie's and Elspeth thought perhaps she could afford to be generous with the space.

"How are you doing?" asked Minnie sympathetically as she settled herself on the sofa with a mug of wine. There weren't any glasses in the flat now - they had all belonged to Peter.

"I'm fine about the breakup," said Elspeth. "Honestly. And I know neither of you liked Peter; maybe you had a point. Anyway, I'm glad we split up when we did."

"Mmm," nodded Ava. "Shame about him taking the lamps, though. I liked those."

"There won't be any plates for dinner either," Elspeth explained. "They were Peter's too. But I've got some saucers, so we can eat off those and just have a little bit at a time."

Minnie and Ava exchanged glances. "Great hosting skills, Elspeth," said Minnie. "So, you said there was something you wanted to talk to us about?"

"Yes. Well. I've got myself into a bit of a ... situation," Elspeth began. She hadn't told them about the job or the flat lease yet. Truth be told, she felt a bit embarrassed about both. "So, it turns out that my current employers won't be extending my contract after my probationary year."

Ava nodded. "I can see why," she commented sagely. "You're not really the lawyer type."

Elspeth wondered whether to enquire *why* Ava felt this was the case, but decided that this probably wasn't the time to pick at that particular thread. "Maybe. Well, anyway, in a few weeks I won't have a job."

"That's really hard," Minnie sympathised. "But I guess you can just look for something else, right?"

"Right. Yes. I can. The only problem is that the lease on the flat runs out in the meantime, so I won't actually have a stable income while I'm looking for a new place to live."

"Ooh. That's a tricky one. Landlords won't touch you with a barge-pole," said Ava helpfully.

"Yes, that's what I thought. So, I was wondering whether either of you might fancy a house guest for a few weeks? You know, just until I get a new job and can find somewhere of my own." Elspeth gave what she hoped was a winning smile that would make her appear an ideal flatmate.

There was a moment of tense silence as Minnie and Ava processed Elspeth's request.

"Well, you know I always want to support you, Elspeth," began Minnie, "but my flat's barely big enough for me as it is. And when we lived together before it ... didn't really go that well, did it?"

"I've told you so many times, Minnie, it wasn't me who stole your cheese. I think you ate it when you were drunk."

"It's not just about the cheese, Elspeth," Minnie explained. "I just think it would put too much pressure on our friendship. And, to be honest, work's pretty intense at the moment and I just need my own space to decompress, you know? I'm sorry, Elspeth, but I can't."

Elspeth took a deep breath. "OK. I understand. Ava? You've got a bigger flat, haven't you? And we've never lived together before – it would be fun!"

"Actually, I can't either," said Ava. "Things are getting a bit more serious with Matt, you know, and he's been staying over quite a bit." She blushed. "I think it might be really going somewhere. We're really enjoying a bit of time just the two of us on the weekends and stuff. I don't want to do anything that might get in the way of it. No offense, Elspeth, but having you sleeping on the sofa would really change the situation. I'm sorry. But listen, hasn't Janice got a spare room?"

Elspeth was crestfallen. Neither of her best friends was willing to help her. When she was in her early twenties, everything had been so much more flexible. Every*one* had been so much more flexible. It hadn't been an issue to sofa surf or live with friends for a bit. Yet now that they were approaching thirty, her friends seemed to be more set in their ways, to want their own space, to be thinking about settling down ... Well, Elspeth couldn't blame them. Two weeks ago *she* had been engaged and trying to settle into a steady job. She wouldn't have wanted Minnie or Ava sleeping on *her* sofa either. Elspeth resolved not to hold it against her friends and to enjoy the rest of the evening as best she could. The ate the curry with its jar-bought sauce on tiny floral saucers using teaspoons, happily polishing off their mugs of wine and listening to the developments on Ava's relationship with Matt, who was a rare choice for Ava in that Minnie and Elspeth didn't actively dislike him. He seemed decent enough and was genuinely interested in getting to know Ava's friends and family. When the girls left around eleven that evening, Elspeth felt far more positive than she had done for a while. Yes, she had lost a fiancée, a job *and* a flat in the last few weeks, but she did have friends. Friends who admittedly wouldn't let her *live* with them, but friends nonetheless.

As Elspeth got ready for bed in the somewhat empty-looking bedroom, devoid as it now was of Peter's belongings, she reflected that it wouldn't be long before she would need to pack up her own items as well. She realised that there was nothing else for it; she would have to call her mother in the morning and throw herself on Janice's charity. Elspeth knew that Janice would at once relish and resent her moving back home for a few weeks. Janice was very clear that she had her own life now, having 'given it up' for eighteen years to raise Elspeth, and would not miss the opportunity to make a point of how intrusive it was to have Elspeth at home again. Yet she would also delight in being needed by Elspeth and would love having a captive audience for her own dramas. Elspeth sighed; it really wasn't a sustainable situation. She would be on the look-out for any possible escape route.

Chapter 5: Eliot and Co.

As predicted, Janice seemed displeased and delighted in equal measure when Elspeth called her to explain her predicament and to ask whether she could move home for a short while.

"Well, it doesn't surprise me. You've never really taken on your adult responsibilities fully, have you, Elspeth? There are a lot of girls your age like that. By the time I was twenty-eight I'd already got married, bought a house with your father and had you - that's *part* of the reason people always assume I'm too young to be your mother, I suppose – we look more like sisters really, although you *have* got your father's nose, unfortunately. Anyway, you can move back in if you need to. It's lucky for you that you've got such a supportive mother. But you'll need to understand that I can't be waiting on you hand and foot – I've got my own life to live, you know. Me and Rick like to have our intimate nights together and I don't want you getting in the way."

Elspeth nearly choked on her cup of tea at the thought of Janice and Rick's *intimate nights*. Rick, a rotund gentleman in his fifties who ran the local newsagents, was a pleasant enough chap, but Elspeth really didn't want to be saddled with *that* particular mental image.

"So," said Elspeth brightly by way of an attempt to settle the matter and close the conversation. "You're OK with me moving in a week on Friday? You'll clear out the spare room for me?"

"I suppose I'll have to," Janice said begrudgingly. "I'd been enjoying it as my crystals room – there's some *very* positive energy in there – but I

44

can't see my own daughter without a place to live, can I?"

"OK. Well, thanks mum, I suppose. That's settled then. I'll bring my things over on Friday evening." Elspeth hung up the phone with a sigh. She knew that she should be grateful to Janice for agreeing to put her up – as she had made abundantly clear, it wasn't necessarily convenient for her. Yet she also found herself resenting the tone of the conversation and the situation in which she found herself. Moving in with Janice was quite literally the *last* thing she wanted to do right now.

It was two days after her conversation with Janice that Elspeth saw a missed call from a number she didn't recognise on her phone. Elspeth had been proactive in contacting letting agents, *just in case* anyone wanted a financially unstable tenant to rent a bargain price one bed flat. Assuming it was one of them calling her back with a rejection, she ignored it. They called again the next day, twice, before leaving a message. Intrigued, Elspeth dialled her voicemail as soon as she got home from work.

"Good afternoon. This is a message for Miss Elspeth Henley. My name is Henry Green of Eliot and Co. Solicitors. We are trying to contact you regarding a bequest made to you in the will of a Reginald Blackwater. Please could you contact our office on ..." The man's voice reeled off a number.

Reginald Blackwater? Who on earth was Reginald Blackwater? Elspeth had never heard the name before in her life. She checked her watch – it was after six o'clock. Presumably the solicitors would be closed for the day. It must be a mistake, she mused. Elspeth Henley wasn't exactly a common name, but presumably there was more than one. Perhaps they had found her number by mistake.

45

Elspeth settled down with a Pot Noodle (she was very grateful that Peter had deigned to leave the kettle) and idly searched online for Reginald Blackwater. She found a few records of various people and some photographs, but no-one she recognised. She resolved to call the solicitors back during her lunch-break the next day; presumably the *real* Elspeth Henley would appreciate being notified of the will.

As Elspeth drifted off to sleep that night, her mind turned over the intriguing idea of a mystery bequest. She wondered what Reginald Blackwater, whoever he was, had left to her namesake Elspeth Henley. Money, probably. But there were so many other possibilities ... antique jewellery, a collection of priceless ornaments, a classic car, even a house! Or maybe something small, a keepsake – a special book or a bundle of love-letters. How romantic that would be. Elspeth fell asleep picturing wooden trunks filled with mysterious packages wrapped in brown paper and tied up with string.

Elspeth took a walk during her lunch hour to give her some privacy to call Eliot and Co. Her call went through to their reception desk, and Elspeth recounted the message she had received notifying her of a bequest, explaining that they must have the wrong person.

"How strange! That's never happened before. Our team are very thorough when they're checking contact details. Did you say it was Henry who called you?"

"Yes."

"Let me just see if he's available now. If it's alright with you I'll put you through to him so we can try to work out what's happened ... Yes, he's available. Just putting you through now."

There was a brief crackle on the line, then a man's voice. "Good morning? I mean afternoon? Is it afternoon? Gosh. Yes it is, already. Sorry. Henry Green here. How can I help you?"

"Good afternoon. This is Elspeth Henley. I received a message from you yesterday regarding a bequest from a Reginald Blackwater."

"Ah yes, Ms Henley. Thank you for calling back. I'm very sorry for your loss."

"For my what? *Oh*, I see. No. That's why I'm calling, actually. There's been some sort of a mistake. I don't know anyone called Reginald Blackwater. You must have got the wrong Elspeth Henley. I thought I should let you know so that you can contact the right one."

There was a moment of silence at the end of the line. "How odd! That's never happened before. Are you sure?"

"Quite sure. Never heard the name Reginald Blackwater in my life."

"Right. Let me look at the file. Well, we definitely have the mobile number that we called you on yesterday on the file. And the home address is ..." Henry read out Elspeth's old address, where Janice still lived.

"Yes," said Elspeth slowly. "That *is* my address ... well, it was ... and it will be again from next week. It's a long story. But where did you get the address from?"

"From Mr Blackwater directly. I took the instructions for his will myself around a year ago. It would appear that you *are* the correct Elspeth Henley. Daughter of Janice Henley?"

Elspeth's eyes widened. How did he know that? "Yes, but ... where did you get that information?"

"Again, from Mr Blackwater directly. There is also a small bequest to Janice Henley."

"Oh!" Elspeth was stunned. So Reginald Blackwater knew her mother. *Interesting*. Janice had presumably had a phone call from Eliot and Co. as well but neglected to mention it. What was she playing at?

"I see. So if I *am* the right Elspeth Henley, then what would I need to do?" she asked.

"Well, you would need to come into our office with appropriate identification documents so that we can verify who you are, then we would proceed to let you know the details of the bequest. We have already contacted the executor of the will and everything looks like it should be fairly straightforward in terms of Mr Blackwater's assets."

"Has my mum already made an appointment to come in?" asked Elspeth, thinking quickly about the best way to outmanoeuvre Janice. "I'm just wondering if it would make sense for us to come in together."

"Yes, that seems sensible. Let's see. She's coming in on Thursday at 4pm. Would that suit you as well, Ms Henley?"

"Perfect. Many thanks for your help, Mr Green. That has been very illuminating."

Elspeth hung up the phone to Mr Green, her curiosity piqued. So there really *was* a mysterious bequest for her! Her mind raced over the possibilities. Almost as intriguing, though, was the fact that Reginald Blackwater, whoever he was, had clearly known Janice – *that* must be his connection to Elspeth – and Janice knew that he had left her something and had already made her appointment with the solicitors. Odd that she hadn't mentioned it. What was she up to? Elspeth checked her watch; she still had fifteen minutes of her lunchbreak left. She dialled Janice's number.

"What's the matter, Elspeth?" Janice was clearly irritated that Elspeth was calling her in the middle of the day. She was presumably very busy doing whatever it was she did all day.

"Nothing, mum," returned Elspeth sweetly. "I was just on my lunch break at work and feeling a bit down, what with losing my fiancée and my job and my flat." Elspeth had decided to lay it on thickly. "So I thought I'd call you to cheer myself up a bit. You know, find out if there's anything going on with you at the moment. Any news of any sort?"

Janice was uncharacteristically silent for a moment. "No," she said. "Nothing going on with me. Just planning the cruise with Margot."

"Oh, right. Yes, it must be nice to have something like that to look forward to. I'd love a holiday, but obviously there's no way I can afford anything like that at the moment. OK, well I wondered whether we could meet up this week one day after work? I'm actually finishing a bit early on Thursday – could you meet me at our usual café for some tea and cake? My treat as a thank you for letting me move back in with you." Elspeth knew this would be a test for Janice. She would never usually turn down an opportunity for tea and cake.

"Thursday ... actually I don't think I can do Thursday, Elspeth. Let's do Saturday morning instead."

"That's a shame. Why can't you do Thursday? What do you have planned?" Elspeth wasn't going to let Janice off gently.

"Erm ..." Janice had never been a particularly accomplished liar. A regular one, perhaps, but not a skilled one. "Margot needs me. That's it. Margot needs me to go clothes shopping with her. She's got terrible taste so she needs me to guide her."

Hmm. So Janice hadn't simply *neglected* to tell Elspeth about her appointment with Eliot and Co. She was deliberately keeping it from her. Elspeth felt utterly justified in her manipulations. "I see. Alright then, we'll go on Saturday instead. I'd better get back to work."

Elspeth returned to her desk, finding it even more difficult than usual to keep her mind on the document bundling as she turned over the possibilities in her mind. One thing was certain: Janice had a secret. It wasn't like her to keep any personal drama to herself – usually she would be boring Elspeth with every little detail. Elspeth found that she had a welcome distraction from her thoughts of Peter, her job and her flat. She couldn't wait to see what revelations Thursday's appointment would bring.

It was a precisely 3.59 pm on Thursday that Elspeth pushed open the smart black front door of Eliot and Co., the gleaming brass sign outside confirming that she had found the right place. She had timed it precisely in order to maximise the extent to which she would disconcert Janice. She knew that her mother was generally ten minutes early for everything, partly so that she didn't have to rush and partly to give her ample time to complain at and generally upset anyone who might be working at the reception desk. Elspeth planned to enter *just* before the time of the appointment, so that her mother would be thoroughly ruffled. It worked. The look on Janice's face as Elspeth calmly entered the waiting room and walked straight to the reception desk, deliberately seeming not to notice Janice, was priceless.

"Hello. Elspeth Henley. I have an appointment with Henry Green regarding the will of Reginald Blackwater."

"Thank you, Ms Henley. He'll just be a moment. Please take a seat."

Elspeth looked around the tiny waiting room as if wondering where to sit, then acted out exaggerated surprise at seeing Janice.

"Mum! What on earth are *you* doing here?"

Janice looked at Elspeth suspiciously. "What are *you* doing here?" she returned, deliberately evading the question.

"Well, it's a *strange* story," said Elspeth, relishing the opportunity to unsettle Janice. "*Apparently* I've been left something in someone's will. The funny thing is, I don't even know him! A Reginald Blackwater. You don't recognise the name, do you mum?" she asked innocently.

Janice went a bit green. Her eyes darted from side to side and Elspeth could almost see the cogs whirring. Could she get away with pretending or was the game up? "Reginald Blackwater ..." she repeated slowly, clearly buying time. "Now, that's a good question ..."

"Mrs Henley? Ms Henley? Would you like to come through together?" A slightly nervous looking man of around Elspeth's age, wearing a brown suit that seemed simultaneously too big and too small for him, was standing awkwardly in the doorway with a pile of files.

"Oh!" said Elspeth pleasantly. "It looks like we must be here about the same thing, mum. We might as well go in together. We are family, after all. It's not as if there are any secrets between *us*, is it?"

Janice looked panicked. "Um ..." was all she could manage.

"Come on then, mum!" Elspeth continued brightly, loving every moment of this. "Let's not keep the nice young man waiting!"

"We're, um, upstairs?" The young man was clearly a frequent user of high rising intonation. It made it sound as if he wasn't quite sure *where* the meeting should take place.

"Great," said Elspeth, following the young man with a wary looking Janice in her wake.

The staircase was narrow and steep, and somehow the young man, who Elspeth assumed was Henry Green, managed to drop the pile of files mid-way up. There was an awkward tangle as he stopped mid-ascent, Elspeth bumping into him and Janice bumping into her, as the files tumbled onto the stair steps, loose papers falling to the floor around their feet.

"Oh dear." Henry looked utterly helpless. "That's rather a problem. I can't actually, er, reach the documents with you there ..."

"Mum, you'll have to reverse," Elspeth explained. With no space to turn around, Janice slowly backed down the stairs, followed by Elspeth, followed by Henry. Once they had reached the bottom, they restarted their ascent, Henry gathering up the papers from the floor as they went. "Sorry about that. Not the best first impression for a client? Well, not that you're my client. Mr Blackwater was? Well. Here we are." At the top of the stairs was a small landing with three doors opening off it. Henry guided them into his office and offered them seats as he placed the files on his desk.

"Right. Sorry, again." His eyes, slightly obscured as they were by his thick, wire-rimmed glasses, looked tired. Elspeth reflected that his job must be even more difficult than her paralegal work. She warmed to him.

"Don't worry, Henry," she said, finding herself using his first name in an attempt to put him at ease. "Those stairs are really quite steep. Thank you very much for taking the time to see us."

"Oh." Henry smiled a little behind his glasses. He clearly wasn't used to be thanked. "That's – well, I mean it's quite literally my job, but still. Thank you for saying that. So, Mr Blackwell's will? I gather you both know already that he has made a bequest to each of you?"

Janice's eyes widened. "He's made a bequest to Elspeth?"

"Yes. Sorry, I thought you knew that. I mean, you *have* spoken about it, I take it?"

"Yes, of course we have! Remember, mum?" Elspeth shot Henry an *Honestly!* look.

Janice nodded silently. She knew when she was beaten.

"Right. So, Mr Blackwater made gifts in his will to both of you: specific legacies." Henry turned his attention to Janice. "To Mrs Janice Henley, I leave my collection of books on British History, my mother's wedding ring, and the sum of four hundred pounds."

Janice's face was a picture. "Really, Reggie?" she said aloud, looking heavenwards. "What on earth do you think I want with a load of books on British History? It was bad enough hearing you banging on about it when you were alive." She shook her head. "But the wedding ring's a nice touch. And the money'll come in handy. Fair enough, Reggie." She nodded, apparently having said everything she needed to on the matter. "So what about her, then?" she asked, nodding to Elspeth.

53

"Okay." Henry gave Elspeth a wide-eyed look, as if to say, *is she always like this?*, which Elspeth returned with a resigned nod. "So, to Ms Elspeth Henley, I leave *The Blue Belle* and all its contents, and the *Blue Belle Fund*, which currently holds the sum of one hundred and fifty five pounds. And eighty-two pence."

Elspeth frowned slightly. "Sorry, I don't understand. What is *The Blue Belle*?"

"Oh. I thought you knew that. Sorry," muttered Henry. "It's a canal boat. A forty-two foot narrow boat, to be precise."

Elspeth's eyes widened. "He's left me a narrow boat? That's – " Elspeth paused. What was it, exactly? Was it odd? Yes. Was it a surprise? Definitely. Was it exciting? Probably. Was it a good thing? She wasn't sure ...

"What kind of, erm, *state* is this boat in?" she asked hesitantly. Elspeth had two mental images in mind: one of a brightly painted, pretty canal boat festooned with flowers, another of a rusting wreck with holes in the roof, abandoned on the British waterways.

"Well, I'm not an expert on canal boats," Henry chuckled, seemingly tickled by the idea that he might be. "But I believe Mr Blackwater was living on the boat himself, so it is habitable."

"Right. Thank you, Henry. Mr Green. This really is a lot to take in."

"Indeed. Well, as I said on the phone, I think the execution of the will should be relatively straightforward, so we will contact you once the bequests are ready to be released and you can, um, get your boat?"

Janice and Elspeth retreated back down the narrow staircase and found themselves outside the polished black door of Eliot and Co. The atmosphere was awkward to say the least. Elspeth was the first to break the silence.

"So, mum. Are you going to tell me who on earth Reginald Blackwater is?" she demanded.

Janice at least had the decency to look a little sheepish. "Well, I didn't think you'd ever need to know about him, Elspeth. How was I to know he'd leave you something in his will? Alright, I'll tell you. But not here; let's go to the café."

Chapter 6: Reggie

Ensconced at a corner table with the biggest, most sugary slice of shortbread she had ever seen, Elspeth took a deep breath. She had to ask the question. "Mum. Was Reginald Blackwater my father?"

Janice raised her eyebrows. "Don't be ridiculous, Elspeth! Of course he wasn't your father! Your father was your father. Where else would you have got that nose?"

Elspeth's hand went self-consciously to her face, as it always did when her mother commented on it. Nobody else seemed to see her nose as particularly problematic, but still.

"No," Janice continued. "And it's Reggie, not Reginald. He hated it when people called him Reginald. Thought it sounded stuck up. No, Reggie's not your father, Elspeth. It was about four years *after* you were born that we became lovers."

Elspeth inadvertently sprayed crumbs from her shortbread all over the table in her coughing fit. She had thought Janice and Rick's *intimate nights* were bad enough, but now she had to hear about Janice's *lover*?

"Your *lover*? Oh, I *really* didn't want to know that. But ... I still don't understand. If Reggie wasn't related to me and his connection was with you, why leave *me* the canal boat?"

Janice shrugged. "You were the only one who ever liked it, I suppose."

Elspeth frowned. She had never met Reggie or seen *The Blue Belle*. Unless ... the memory washed over her like a wave, the details like little snapshots of moments in time. A towpath on a rainy day. Climbing onto a wooden plank to get onto a boat. A man's large hand reaching out to help her steady herself. A tattoo on the man's forearm: an anchor. Playing hide and seek inside a boat. The pictures had always been there, Elspeth realised, but she hadn't been sure whether they really were a memory or just some photographs she had seen or even a story she had been told.

"Mum, did Reggie have an tattoo of an anchor on his forearm?"

Janice looked up momentarily from her Victoria sponge. "Yes, he did. So you remember him, then? I'm surprised. Thought you were too young to remember that."

"Yes." Elspeth scoured her memory for more details. "And the inside of the boat; there was a kind of wooden planking on the walls – almost like a sauna – and a dark red patterned carpet."

Janice nodded. "That's right. It's probably still like that as far as I know. Reggie wasn't the interior decorating type. Can't imagine him doing much with it."

Elspeth felt a stirring of excitement. The memories of the canal boat – *The Blue Belle* – were already in her and gave her a warm, comforting feeling when she thought about them. But she had more questions.

"I don't understand, though, mum. You said Reggie was your ..." Elspeth gulped hard and tried to keep her shortbread down, "lover. So why was *I* visiting the boat in the first place?"

"Teacher training days," said Janice simply.

"But ... hang on ..." Elspeth thought about the timeline. Judging from the haziness of the memory, she must have been at infant school when they visited *The Blue Belle*. "You and dad were still married then, mum."

Janice didn't even have the decency to look uncomfortable. "Yes. So?"

"So what were you playing at, taking your daughter to visit your lover while you were still married?"

"Didn't make any difference to you or your dad, did it? He didn't care what I was doing all day. And me and Reggie always met on Mondays – the teacher training days must've been Mondays I suppose – and there was no point cancelling on him. And I thought you'd like to see the boat. You were always very bored and annoying as a child; it gave me something to do with you for the day."

Elspeth sat back in her chair and regarded Janice as one might a rare, perhaps unpredictable species in the wild. She didn't understand this woman in the slightest. To take her daughter to visit her lover on teacher training days, while she was still married. Honestly. Much as Elspeth really didn't want to know more of the murky details, she had to get a clearer picture of what had happened. It still seemed odd that Reggie had left her the boat after only meeting her a few times.

"So, you and Reggie. Was it a long term thing? Was it serious?"

"I suppose it was," said Janice, a nostalgic expression on her face. "He was head over heels for me, that's for sure. Made a change from your father who wouldn't have noticed if I'd walked in the room starkers."

"Mum!" Yet another mental picture courtesy of Janice that Elspeth couldn't un-imagine. "OK, so tell me about it. How did you meet?"

"We met at a pub," Janice said. "There was an event on, a local band playing, so I'd got myself a bit dressed up. You remember that blue dress I used to have? The one you called my princess dress." Elspeth did remember. A creation in chiffon with a bit of sparkle. She had loved it as a child and desperately wanted to be big enough to wear it. Of course, once she *was* big enough, she wouldn't have touched it with a barge-pole. "Well, I was wearing that," Janice continued. "That's when Reggie noticed me. *The blue belle of the ball*, he called me."

The blue belle of the ball. *The Blue Belle.* "So the boat's named after you?"

"Yep. Reggie bought it about a year after we met and changed the name when he re-painted it. Named it after me. I suppose I was the love of his life," said Janice grandly.

"So why not leave it to you, then? Why to me instead?"

"Oh, I hate boats," said Janice. "Can't stand them. Pokey, rickety little things. Hardly space to stand up properly. But those times I took you, you couldn't get enough of it. Asking all these questions, wanting to touch the steering thing, whatever you call it. Messing about inside the boat playing hide and seek. You told Reggie you wanted to live on a canal boat of your own when you were a grown up and he said that you could have *The Blue Belle* one day. He always remembered it. Sentimental type he was, sometimes. I didn't think he was serious, to be honest. But here we are. And now *I've* got to work out what to do with all his British history books. Still, nice that he left me the wedding ring, though." Janice smiled to herself at the thought, while Elspeth sipped her warm mug of tea and reflected on her situation. It had been an interesting afternoon, to say the least; she would soon be the owner of a canal boat. Elspeth had lost so many things over the past few weeks: her relationship, her job and, soon enough, her flat. There was certainly space in her life for something new to come in. She just hadn't thought for a moment that it would be a forty-two foot narrow boat.

Chapter 7: *The Blue Belle*

It was around two weeks after their meeting with Henry Green that Elspeth saw *The Blue Belle* for the first time. It was moored around four miles from the small semi-detached house where she was now living, inharmoniously, with Janice, having moved all of her things into Janice's spare room the week before. Janice had agreed to accompany Elspeth to go and see the boat, and for once Elspeth was genuinely glad to have her along for the ride. She had never been to the place that the narrow boat was moored and had no idea what to expect. Somehow having Janice with her, who had clearly spent lots of time on *The Blue Belle* with Reggie, made it feel less daunting. And, uncomfortable as she was with the thought, Janice was Elspeth's connection to Reggie and to the narrow boat. She felt, somehow, that Reggie and *The Blue Belle* would like her to bring Janice along. Parking her car near to the towpath, Elspeth and Janice made their way towards the boat's mooring.

"There she is," said Janice, as a blue and white narrow boat came into view.

She, thought Elspeth. *Of course she's a she.* Elspeth suddenly felt almost shy, as if she were meeting a new acquaintance and was nervous about whether they'd like her.

Elspeth approached the small boat, taking in as many details as she could. It certainly wasn't the leaking, rusting wreck that she had feared, yet it wasn't the pretty picture postcard narrow boat of her dreams either. From the outside, the boat seemed to be in sound but not loved condition. The paintwork was flaking and peeling a little, but the blue was still vibrant and the legend *The Blue Belle* was clearly visible, emblazoned as it was across the side of the boat in a white brush script. The window sills looked a little rusty, but watertight, and the little wooden plank that linked the boat to the towpath seemed sturdy enough.

"Well, go on then," urged Janice impatiently. "I'm meeting Margot for lunch; I can't spend all day faffing about on a towpath."

Elspeth gingerly climbed aboard before turning back to help Janice. As she held out her hand to her mother, her mind flicked back to the image of her own hand reaching out for the great paw of the man with the anchor tattoo on his forearm. Reggie. *Welcome aboard.*

Elspeth had been given the keys to the boat via Henry at Eliot and Co., and now she slipped one into the lock of the door that would lead to the boat's interior. The door itself was wooden and, at five foot eight, Elspeth had to duck slightly to enter the cabin. She felt nervous as she opened the door; what kind of state would Reggie have left his living quarters in?

The first thing to greet Elspeth was the smell. It wasn't *wholly* unpleasant, but the boat certainly smelled 'lived in'. Reggie clearly hadn't been a great enthusiast when it came to domestic tasks. The interior was dark; the wooden panelling that Elspeth remembered from her childhood visits to the boat still covered the walls and ceiling, making the small space feel even more enclosed. And the stuff! There wasn't a great deal of floor space to play with in the first place, but almost every inch was covered with piles of books, magazines, paperwork, abandoned coffee mugs, plates, clothes, boots ... Elspeth remembered

62

the wording of the bequest: *To Ms. Elspeth Henley, I leave The Blue Belle and all of its contents.* Elspeth wasn't sure exactly what she had been hoping the contents might include: perhaps a pretty tea set or a comfy sofa. Instead, it appeared she had been gifted some dirty laundry, a pile of washing up and several trips to the local tip.

Busy absorbing the details of her acquisition, Elspeth hadn't noticed Janice's response to being back on the boat. Now, she saw, Janice had squeezed past Elspeth to go to the curtained off area at the back of the boat that presumably served as a bedroom. Elspeth followed Janice, to find her sitting on the edge of the compact bed, surrounded by Reggie's discarded items, a melancholy expression on her face. Elspeth realised that this was a rare moment of genuine emotion for Janice. In all the strangeness of the situation, Elspeth hadn't really considered Janice's emotional reaction to coming back here. Elspeth sat next to her on the bed, which creaked slightly under their combined weight.

"Does it feel strange, coming back here?" Elspeth asked gently.

Janice nodded. "Had some good times in this bed," she said, wiping a tear from her eye. Elspeth decided now was not the time to be appalled by her mother's lack of tact. "Reggie used to call me his princess. We'd always have a garibaldi afterwards. He loved his garibaldis."

Unsure whether she wanted to know the answer, Elspeth had to ask: "sorry, what's a *garibaldi*?"

"It's a type of biscuit. Got currants in it," Janice sniffed. "Don't they teach you anything at University? Anyway, it just feels strange being here without him. This whole place is so ... Reggie."

For once, Elspeth agreed utterly with Janice's sentiments. Being in this space, she could almost feel Reggie's character. There was warmth here, and strength, but she also sensed that Reggie would not have been a man to compromise.

"I get the impression Reggie was someone who lived life on his own terms," Elspeth ventured. "Is that right?"

Janice looked at her curiously. "That's exactly right," she said. "It's funny – it's almost as if you knew him yourself. That was partly why we ended things when we did. He wanted to be free to travel around on this thing," she gestured to *The Blue Belle*, "and he wanted me to go with him! Can you imagine, me living on a boat?" Mercifully, Elspeth couldn't imagine it. "So I told him he'd better go off and do it on his own. And that I wouldn't be sat here waiting for him."

"Well, you *were* also still married to dad, so technically you wouldn't have been waiting ..."

"Well, *technically*. But anyway, me and Reggie went our separate ways. Most of the time. But he'd come back now and again and we'd, you know ..."

Elspeth's eyes widened. "Really? Until when?"

Janice shrugged. "Last May was the last one. Right here." She nodded to the bed.

Privately resolving to replace the mattress as soon as possible, Elspeth tried to remain supportive.

"I'll do my best with it, you know," she said. "I'll make sure that anything I find of Reggie's that might be, you know, sentimental, I'll show you and see if you want to keep it. And I'll try to look after *The Blue Belle*; keep it as something he'd be proud of."

Janice nodded. "You're a good girl, Elspeth," she said. It was probably the biggest compliment she had ever given her.

Janice busied herself looking through some items in the bedroom while Elspeth explored the rest of the boat. It was, as Janice had suggested, seemingly mostly untouched since Elspeth's childhood visits. The décor was very dated, and the small squares of carpet that Elspeth *could* see beneath the mountains of mess were clearly filthy and worn. The tiny wooden kitchen was just about serviceable – there was no oven, but there was a little hob and a kettle; there was no dishwasher, but there was a practical sink. The tiny shower-room was decked out in avocado and was very basic, but again, seemed to be in working order. Elspeth noticed a small wood burner which, she hoped, might still be usable. The whole interior would need a great deal of work and Elspeth was nervous at the extent of it, but as Henry from Eliot and Co. had said, the narrow boat *was* habitable.

Excited by her findings of that afternoon, Elspeth had arranged to meet Minnie and Ava for a drink at their local pub, *The Duck Inn*. Besides wanting to share the news of her first viewing of *The Blue Belle*, there was the added incentive that Rick was visiting Janice that evening and Elspeth certainly did *not* want to bear witness to their blossoming romance. No; Janice needed her own space, and so did Elspeth. Minnie arrived before Ava and joined Elspeth at their window table, where Elspeth had already made a start on their first bottle of cold white wine and a sharing bag of crisps.

"So, today was the big boat viewing day!" said Minnie, pouring herself a generous glass of wine and clinking glasses with Elspeth. "To *The Blue Belle*!"

Elspeth smiled broadly. It really did feel like she had something to celebrate after weeks of disappointment. "Thanks, Minnie. It was so good to see it in reality today; I just couldn't imagine what it was like, you know?"

"I'm here!" Ava slid onto the banquette next to Elspeth. "Wine. Amazing. Cheers! So, what news of your canal boat?"

"Well, I think it's pretty good, actually," Elspeth said cautiously. She didn't want to get ahead of herself, but the boat certainly seemed to be an asset rather than an issue. 'It's going to need a lot of work," she said. "The inside's really dated and there's a lot of old junk in there, but it *looks* sound. Apparently it's a good idea to get a survey done when you're taking on a boat, just to see if there are any major issues. It'll cost about five hundred pounds, apparently, but I think it's worth doing to check there are no major issues before I start working on it."

Ava raised her eyebrows. "Wow. Things are moving quickly, Elspeth! What do you mean, *working on it*? Sounds like you've got a plan."

Elspeth nodded shyly. It had been forming in her mind from the moment Henry the solicitor had revealed the nature of the bequest. "Well, I've been thinking about it a lot. I mean, I could sell *The Blue Belle*, but that wouldn't feel right. Reggie left it to me because he thought I wanted it. Admittedly, that thought was based on a casual conversation with my seven year old self, but still ... I feel selling it would be somehow dishonest. Does that make sense?"

"Kind of," said Minnie, "but it's not as if Reggie will actually *know* what you do with it. And it is quite a commitment to be responsible for a narrow boat. If you did sell it, would it be worth a bit?"

Elspeth nodded. "I've been doing a bit of research. In its current state, I think it'd be worth somewhere around the twenty to twenty-five thousand mark," she revealed.

"Woah! That's a lot more than I thought," Ava exclaimed. "I mean, I get what you're saying about the spirit of the bequest and everything, but that kind of money could give you a house deposit! Just think what you could do with the money, Elspeth."

Elspeth nodded. She *had* thought about it. But her mind was made up. She was going to trust her instincts this time.

"Yes. I have thought about it. A lot. And having that kind of money would definitely open up possibilities for me. But there's another way to think about it. Imagine if I never even *need* to buy a house! Or rent an over-priced flat ever again! Imagine if I can have somewhere to live, practically rent free, for as long as I like! And *wherever* I like!" Elspeth beamed at her friends, confident that they would be as convinced and enchanted as she was with the possibility.

Ava and Minnie exchanged worried glances.

"Is she saying she's going to live on a barge for the rest of her life?" Minnie whispered.

Ava nodded, glancing surreptitiously at Elspeth. "I think she is. Do you think she's OK? She *has* been under quite a lot of stress recently."

"Seriously, you have to stop doing this. I can *hear* you!" Elspeth interjected.

Ava took a deep breath. "You know, Elspeth," she began, in the tone of someone trying to calmly reason with a lunatic, "most people don't *live* on barges. They might go on holiday on them for a week, but then they go back to their *homes*. Which have things like *rooms*. And *hallways*. Maybe even *stairs*. And ceilings that you don't bump your head on."

Elspeth gave Ava what she hoped was a cold, hard stare. "I'm fully aware of that, Ava. But that's partly because most people don't think outside the box, you know? We're given this set of aspirations and expectations about how people live in our culture and we take them on unquestioningly. But ... well, I've been *forced* to think outside the box and the more I consider it, the more I think that living on a barge would be amazing. I've got a lot to learn in order to make it work, I know that. I've no idea how you .. drive one? Pilot one? Charter one? I'm not even sure what the right term is. But I can learn about all of that. And in the meantime, it would give me so much freedom! I'm finishing my paralegal job next week and I've got nothing else lined up. There aren't many opportunities out there and I won't exactly have a glowing reference from my old firm. So I'll have to pick up some casual work rather than something salaried, I guess. But if my income isn't that high, just imagine not having to meet a regular rent payment every month! I know there are costs with running a narrow boat, for mooring and such like, but I'm sure it won't be as much as a rental payment. It's ... well, it's liberating. Reggie had the right idea."

Minnie shrugged. "Maybe in the summer it'll be OK, Elspeth," she said reasonably, "but what about the winter months? It'll be freezing. And whereas in the summer you can get out and about a bit, in the winter you'll just want to hunker down sometimes. You won't have any *space*, Elspeth. I'd go stir crazy."

Elspeth nodded. She'd thought about that too. "Well, I'll just have to wrap up warm and go for winter walks or something. I'll find a way. Some people *do* live on narrow boats all year round, so it must be possible. And let's face it," Elspeth continued glumly, "I can't stay with Janice for much longer."

Ava pulled a face. "Intimate night with Rick again?"

Elspeth nodded. "I'm not going home until we get thrown out of here at closing time," she said. "And when I get home, I'm going straight to bed with my ear plugs in."

Chapter 8: Nina

It was Elspeth's last day in her paralegal role, and she felt a little deflated as she packed her small collection of personal possessions into a cardboard box in order to clear her desk towards the end of the afternoon. Nina had barely spoken to Elspeth since their meeting in which it had become clear that Elspeth's contract would not be renewed. She was therefore a little surprised when Nina called her into her office around an hour before she was planning to leave.

Elspeth sensed a difference in Nina's demeanour the moment she entered her office. Rather than sitting in her usual power chair behind her desk, Nina was perched on the small corner sofa in her swanky office. Elspeth had never actually seen anyone *sit* on it before; she had assumed it was there more for the look of the thing than for actual use. Elspeth noticed a packet of unopened chocolate digestives on the adjacent coffee table.

"Nina? You wanted to see me?"

"Yes! Hi Elspeth. Come in."

"Okay," Elspeth said warily, feeling like she was entering the lion's den. Nina gestured to the sofa beside her, and Elspeth perched warily on the edge of it.

"Would you like a biscuit?" asked Nina awkwardly.

"Maybe," replied Elspeth suspiciously.

"Right. I'll open them. There." Nina offered one to Elspeth then took one herself.

"So, I suppose you're wondering why I've asked you to come and see me?" said Nina.

Elspeth nodded. "Well, I think I've done all of the formal stuff with HR and clearly you won't be giving me any more work, so I *was* a bit surprised."

Nina nodded. Elspeth realised that she was nervous. "Is everything OK, Nina?" she asked.

Nina nodded again, then shook her head. "Actually, no. It isn't really. It never is. It's just *so hard*, Elspeth." And with that, iron Nina put her head in her hands and sobbed.

"There, there," Elspeth consoled, awkwardly patting Nina on the shoulder. 'Here, have a tissue." She pulled one from the box on Nina's desk.

"Thank you." Nina blew her nose loudly. "That's better. Well, the thing is, Elspeth, that I'm having a really difficult time at the moment. Well, when I say *at the moment*, I really mean for the last three years since I split up with my partner."

"Oh!" was all Elspeth could manage. She wasn't used to this kind of personal sharing from Nina.

"You see, I have three children, Elspeth. Three! Seb's eight, Katherine's five and Ollie's three. I have full custody and I'm the sole breadwinner. My ex-husband was – well, he wasn't a very nice guy, really. He doesn't have a job and he doesn't want anything to do with the children, so ..." she trailed off.

"That's really hard, Nina," sympathised Elspeth. "You do amazingly, you know," she said. "Being so professional at work, working the hours that you do. I don't know how you manage it." Elspeth genuinely meant what she said; she could barely get things together enough to support herself, let alone three children. "But, Nina, I'm struggling to see what this has to do with me. Are you looking for a nanny or something?"

Nina burst out laughing. "No! I have a perfectly competent nanny already, thank goodness. And, no offence, but I probably wouldn't leave *you* in charge of three children for hours on end. No, Elspeth. I don't want a nanny." Nina took a deep breath. "I want a friend."

At Elspeth's look of wide-eyed surprise, Nina continued. "Look, it might sound odd to you, but when I was looking at your file the other week, I realised something. We're the same age, Elspeth! And I thought how strange it was that we were at such different places in our lives. And then I thought that it must be fun to ... well, to be *you* sometimes. To go for drinks with friends. To not have to take work so seriously. To have a bit of fun!" Nina broke off to blow her nose loudly again. "I don't remember the last time I had any fun, Elspeth. And the really pathetic thing is, I don't have anyone to have any fun *with*! I'm not in touch with my school friends or my University friends anymore and I never got to know the school mums because I'm not there for the school run or the social events. I even thought about joining one of those apps, kind of like dating apps but for friends, but it seemed too pathetic. And then I thought, now that you're leaving and I won't be your boss anymore, maybe ... maybe you could be my friend?"

Elspeth was speechless. She felt like she was back in her primary school playground. Nobody had asked her outright to be their friend since she was six! It wasn't how adults usually went about things; Nina's approach was clearly unconventional, but that wasn't necessarily a *bad* thing. Yet there was something Elspeth couldn't understand.

"Nina," she said. "I'm perfectly open to the idea of us being friends – well, trying to be friends at least and seeing how it goes – but there's just one thing bothering me about the idea."

"OK. What?"

"Well," Elspeth paused. "You don't actually seem to *like* me. I mean, since I've been working here, you've never spoken to me socially at all, whenever you've given me work to do you've always been a bit offish with me, and then you decided not to renew my probationary contract. I mean, it doesn't exactly scream friendship, does it?"

Nina blew her nose loudly again. "Sorry about that," she said, depositing the soggy tissue on the coffee table where Elspeth eyed it warily. "The thing is, Elspeth, I *don't* like you as an employee. Not in this kind of role, anyway. You're chatty, you're always talking about your life outside work, you find the work boring, you always give the impression that you'd rather be off somewhere else doing something more fabulous ... *and* you're charismatic, so your colleagues find you distracting and want to talk to you rather than getting *their* work done. And don't get me started on your effect on some of your male colleagues."

"My effect?"

"They're like puppies when you're around." Nina assumed a pathetic, doe-eyed look. "Oh Elspeth, let me carry those heavy files for you ... Oh Elspeth, please can I leave my wife and eat cookies with you all day ... Oh Elspeth, let's ditch our boring corporate lives and run away together ... I mean, obviously that's not the reason I didn't renew your contract. *That* was because you're always late and you don't get your work done by the deadlines, which is *kind of* important in a law firm. But still ... you're far too interesting to be conducive to a productive working environment in a place like this."

Elspeth sat back in surprise. Nina had said she was *charismatic* and *interesting*. Used as she was to Janice's constant digging, Elspeth would take a compliment where she could get it. Now that Nina mentioned it, Elspeth could see what she meant about some of her male colleagues: Michael from Accounts and Neil from Tax in particular. Neil had *quite literally* fallen over himself the other day trying to simultaneously open a door for her while insisting he carry her boxes through. The firm had needed to update their health and safety policy as a result. Poor Neil.

"So you see," Nina continued, "the very things that make you a terrible fit as a paralegal at a law firm would make you a brilliant friend to have! People warm to you. You can talk to anyone. You're interesting on a social level." Nina looked downcast for a moment. "I know that I'm not those things. Not anymore. People don't warm to me. They think I'm hard. Well, I am these days, I suppose. I've forgotten how to talk about anything other than work. I'm not interesting to anyone outside of this law firm. I need someone to shake me out of it, to introduce me to people, to remind me that I can still enjoy myself. So, what do you think?"

Elspeth eyed Nina's hopeful yet insecure expression and smiled broadly. "Yes! Of course we can be friends, Nina. Well, I mean, we can try it and see how it goes. I'll tell you what; I'm going for a drink with my friends Minnie and Ava tonight. How about you join us? Eight o'clock at *The Duck Inn*."

"Tonight? Well, Seb's got football and Katherine's got ballet but we could be back by seven ... I'm sure my neighbour's daughter could babysit.

I'll text her now and ask. OK, Elspeth. Babysitter pending, you're on!"

As Elspeth carried the boxes to her car an hour later, she reflected that, actually, she really hadn't done that badly at the law firm after all. Yes, she now knew that it wasn't the right field for her, but at least she'd tried. It had given her a year of relative financial stability to help her to get herself back on track, and she was leaving a little bit richer than she had started. Not only had she slipped a few extra post-it notes and a couple of pens into her cardboard box; she had also gained a friend.

Chapter 9: Home Sweet Home

Elspeth quite literally couldn't wait to move out of Janice's spare room: she was counting down the days until moving onto *The Blue Belle* would be a possibility. She had always found her mother difficult to live with to say the least, and returning home as a twenty-eight year old, having lived mostly independently since the age of eighteen, the dynamic was impossible. Elspeth had decided to wait until she'd had *The Blue Belle* surveyed to check that it was sound, then, provided the boat seemed safe enough, she planned to move aboard regardless of its internal condition.

Meeting the surveyor, William, one Friday morning, Elspeth was full of trepidation at what he might find. Her whole plan hinged on there not being any major problems with the boat. Any significant issues with the hull would be expensive to fix, she knew, and she wasn't sure quite where she would find the money to do that kind of work. Elspeth definitely didn't want to get herself into debt again; it had taken a lot of discipline to dig herself out of that particular hole. Thankfully, William was helpful and knowledgeable. He told Elspeth that the shell of *The Blue Belle* had clearly been well maintained, and the hull was in good condition for a narrow boat of its age. Elspeth was delighted. William gave her a few useful pointers on aspects of the narrow boat she might want to address when she had the money and the opportunity: there were some minor issues with rust around the joins above the waterline and the window frames could do with being replaced eventually, but essentially the boat was sound. The whole thing would, of course, benefit from a new coat of exterior paint and some aspects of the interior were in need an upgrade, but the boat was certainly safe and habitable.

Elspeth thanked William for his help and found herself full of enthusiasm for the next stage of her plan. It would be hard graft, she knew, but she was determined that she would move onto *The Blue Belle* that week and would begin work on the interior herself. Elspeth's art degree had given her some valuable skills in wood and metal work. Admittedly, she had previously only done welding and carpentry as a means to create sculptural pieces, but she reasoned that the principles would be the same. She was confident using tools and working with materials; she had just never done anything on this kind of scale. She knew that she could learn.

Currently between jobs as she was, Elspeth had time to focus on her project. She thought carefully about what she wanted to take with her onto *The Blue Belle* and realised that this was the start of a new chapter for her. The previous chapter of her life, the one in which she had been a paralegal, living in a smart ground floor flat with her fiancée, was now closed, but Elspeth began to feel that this was a *good* thing. She couldn't in all honesty say that she had been altogether happy in that version of her life, or that she had felt true to herself. She now had a chance to do something utterly different; to *live* in a way that was utterly different. As she packed up her belongings, she began to question what she really wanted to take into this new stage of her life. Space on *The Blue Belle* would be limited, and, for the first few months at least, she would essentially be living on a building site. Elspeth thought carefully about what she really wanted to keep with her, realising that she didn't want to fill this new chapter of her life with all of her old *stuff*. Looking through the bin bags full of clothes, books and other items that she had accumulated over the years, Elspeth reflected that most of this wouldn't suit her new lifestyle, anyway. She would need practical clothes for doing the work on *The Blue Belle* and warm clothes and blankets for the winter months. Her piles of fashionable outfits for work and socialising seemed suddenly redundant. Elspeth knew that it wasn't fair to use Janice's house as a storage facility – Janice was clearly pleased at the prospect of re-instating her crystals room - so she packed the boot of her car with several bags for the charity shop. She would only take the things she really wanted and needed onto *The Blue Belle*. She wanted to begin this chapter with a sense of lightness; to make space for new adventures.

Having dropped off her bags at the charity shop, Elspeth found that moving the remainder of her things out of Janice's spare room didn't take long. Later that afternoon, her car packed with the belongings she would be keeping, she felt ready to make the move. Elspeth knew that Minnie and Nina would both be swamped at work, but Ava's job as a self-employed marketing contractor was a little more flexible. She called her.

"Ava! Is now a good time?"

"Yes, it's fine, Elspeth. I'm just trying to put together a presentation for a client, but I could do with a break."

"Well, that's just why I was calling! Any chance you could take a break for an hour or two?"

"Probably. As long as I get it to the client by the end of the week they won't mind. Why, what are you thinking? Tea and cake?"

"Well, we could do that too. But actually, I wondered whether you'd come with me to *The Blue Belle*. I'm going to ... well, I'm going to move in this afternoon. It just feels a bit odd doing it on my own. I'd really appreciate some company."

"Ooh! Yes, I'd love to. I haven't seen it yet. I'm intrigued. OK. Text me the postcode for where to park and I'll meet you there."

Elspeth arrived at the road near the towpath first, and waited in her car for a few minutes until she saw Ava's smart BMW pull up.

"I've never been anywhere like this before," said Ava as they walked towards the mooring. "I *think* I like it. It feels like we've time travelled back to the 1960s or something."

"I know what you mean," said Elspeth. "There's something ... traditional about it, isn't there? OK," Elspeth paused for effect. "Here she is!"

'Oh! Not as bad as I thought," ventured Ava. "She needs a coat of paint, but she looks quite sweet, really."

"See? I *told* you that me moving onto *The Blue Belle* is a good idea. Come on in."

Elspeth unlocked the door of the narrow boat and the girls stepped down into the narrow, dark space. "So, what do you think?" asked Elspeth.

At first she thought Ava hadn't heard her, due to the total silence from her friend. Elspeth turned to look at Ava and saw an expression of utter horror.

"You can't be *serious*, Elspeth," said Ava, wrinkling her nose. "This is tiny! And dark. And smelly. And ... well ... *horrible*." Ava looked around her in disgust. "Maybe when it's been re-fitted you could consider staying here for a bit, but in *this* state ..." she trailed off.

Elspeth felt deflated. Maybe Ava was right. She looked at the interior of *The Blue Belle* with fresh eyes; it *was* a pretty unappealing prospect. But so was the idea of Janice and Rick's *intimate nights*.

Taking a deep breath, Elspeth feigned confidence. "Oh, it's only cosmetic! A bit of paint and some rugs and it'll be cosy as anything. You'll see!"

Ava nodded uncertainly. "Maybe. Sorry, Elspeth, I should be more positive about it for your sake. Come on, let's get the rest of your stuff from the car."

Together, Elspeth and Ava spent the next hour emptying the car of Elspeth's belongings and doing their best to organise them in a sensible way on the narrow boat. The truth was, there wasn't much space, what with all of Reggie's personal possessions still covering every inch of the surface and floor. Once they had moved all of Elspeth's items on board, Elspeth found the kettle that Peter had allowed her to keep and the girls made a cup of tea which they took outside, sitting on the small seats on the prow of *The Blue Belle*. Ava had bought some cookies with her for them to share; it was a beautiful, bright day, and the sunlight warmed them as they drank their tea and ate their treats. There was plenty to see from their vantage point on the canal: pretty boats gliding up and down, people walking dogs or jogging along the towpath, the movement of the sparkling water and the gentle scudding of the light clouds.

"You know, Elspeth," said Ava, "I really *am* sorry about what I said when I first saw inside your boat. I mean, it does need a lot of work, but if anyone can do it, you can."

Elspeth warmed at the unexpected compliment. Ava wasn't usually this sensitive.

"And I can see the appeal," continued Ava. "It's beautiful out here. I've been thinking a lot about what I want out of life, you know, what with things getting more serious with Matt. I think I *do* want a pretty conventional life; maybe to get married in the next couple of years, buy a house, have children one day. But I don't think that's the only route to happiness. And, to be honest, you haven't seemed that happy for the last couple of years. Me and Minnie didn't want to say anything, but being with Peter, working at that law firm – it kind of ..." Ava searched for the right word, "*squashed* you a bit. Took some of the light out of you."

Elspeth nodded. She hadn't realised it at the time; she had just thought she was being sensible and doing what adults were supposed to do. But now that she thought about it, Ava was absolutely right. She had stifled something in herself these last three years. Giving up her art, donning a suit, spending her evenings watching documentaries with Peter; it just wasn't *her*. "You're right, Ava," she said. "Why didn't you and Minnie say anything?"

"Well, from my perspective, I didn't really know what I could say. *I* don't have any answers; I'm only just figuring out what I should do with myself! The thing is, the path you were on before you met Peter wasn't working either; getting yourself into debt and having those relationships with other artists who mostly slept on people's sofas ... so perhaps it was good to have a bit of time going the other way. Maybe now's a time to find a different path altogether, you know?"

It made sense. It wasn't a stark choice between being a broke artist or a sensible lawyer. There *were* other options.

"Anyway, I'd better get going," said Ava. "Thanks, Elspeth. That was actually a really nice break from preparing my presentation. See you at the pub on Friday."

Once Ava had left, Elspeth went back into the main living area of *The Blue Belle*. It was the first time that she had been in there alone – previously, she had only viewed the boat with Janice, then the surveyor, and now Ava. Perching in a small patch of uncluttered space on the grimy, hard sofa in the saloon, she surveyed her new home. Gosh, this was going to be a lot of work. Well, no time like the present. It was three o'clock; Elspeth realised there were at least three working hours left in the day. If she was going to see restoring *The Blue Belle* as her job for the time being, she'd better clock on.

Rummaging in one of the cardboard boxes for her small radio, Elspeth put it on and immediately felt the atmosphere in the boat change. She smiled to herself. Thanks to Reggie, this was going to be her space. She would start making herself at home. Knowing the extent of the clear-out she would need to undertake, Elspeth had brought several rolls of bin bags with her: black for rubbish, white for possible donations and green for recycling. She got started on the surface clutter first. Filling the sink with warm water and a generous dollop of washing up liquid, she placed all of the dirty dishes, cups and glasses she could find into the water. Some of the items would probably not be salvageable, she knew, untouched for weeks as they had been, but she wanted to try. Next, she set about picking up anything that was clearly rubbish: wrappers, containers, random bits and bobs that had clearly been discarded. The following stage would be more difficult, she knew: items for donation. Clearly nothing on *The Blue Belle* could be donated in its current condition, and there was no washing machine on board the boat. Elspeth planned to make a trip to the local laundrette the next day to wash all of Reggie's clothes before working out what could be donated to charity for re-sale and what would need to go to textile recycling. For now, she gathered up all of the clothing items which were strewn everywhere on *The Blue Belle*: on the surfaces in the galley, in the berth, in the saloon, even on the floor of the small shower room; and corralled them into four white bin bags, which she decided to stow in the boot of her car overnight to give her more space on board.

It was past eight o'clock when Elspeth, exhausted and grubby-feeling after her exertions, stood at the sink scrubbing the last of the dirty pots. Most of them had come up surprisingly well after their long soak, and there were only a few items that she didn't think she could salvage. She looked around the interior of the boat: it felt so much more spacious after her efforts. Now she just needed to make up the bed with the bedding she had brought with her (she realised grimly that replacing the mattress that Janice and Reggie had enjoyed such good times on would have to wait for now) and then she could cosy up for the night. Elspeth took the old bedding off the mattress and, trying very hard to ignore the state of the mattress itself, placed her fresh under-sheet and pretty duvet and pillows on it. There. It looked and smelt fresh and inviting. Delighting in the fact that she would not have to wake up to an alarm and could have a leisurely breakfast before visiting the laundrette in the morning, Elspeth read for an hour before falling into a deep sleep, lulled by the gentle rocking of *The Blue Belle* on the water.

Chapter 10: Unreasonable Barge Man

Unfortunately, Elspeth's hopes for restorative night's sleep and a leisurely breakfast were not to be realised. The beautifully warm summer day turned into an unbearably humid night, and in her exhausted state Elspeth couldn't manage to open the small metal framed windows on *The Blue Belle*, as the mechanisms seemed to be stuck through lack of use. Tossing and turning in her bed, Elspeth began to feel like she was trapped inside a little tin box, with no fresh air and no way to keep cool. She dozed off a few times, but her sleep was fitful. Lying awake and thinking that the night couldn't get any worse, Elspeth heard a rumble in the distance. Of course. The weather was about to break. It was around five in the morning that the storm began.

The thunder approached slowly and menacingly, and Elspeth felt suddenly very vulnerable on the little boat. She didn't know anything about canal boats other than the information she had gleaned from William, the surveyor, and had no idea how *The Blue Belle* would fare in a storm. What if it came loose from its mooring and drifted down the canal? She didn't even know how to switch on the engine, let alone steer it! What if there were leaks in the roof and the water came in? What if the boat sank? Catastrophising as the thunder and lightning moved closer until the storm was almost directly over the small craft, Elspeth buried her face in her pillow as the heavens opened and rain lashed at the sides of *The Blue Belle*, the wind buffeting it and the thunder rolling overhead. Elspeth was terrified. It was a wonder that she managed to sleep at all, but she realised she must have done, as she was rudely awoken by shouting outside *The Blue Belle*.

The thunder and lightning had subsided, but the rain continued to come down in sheets. Her heart racing in response to the unexpected interruption and her continued alarm at the storm, Elspeth raised her face to the bedroom window to see a man standing on the towpath near *The Blue Belle*, dressed in a high vis jacket and trousers, an enormous high vis rainhat pulled down over his face. He was shouting and gesturing; it took Elspeth a moment to realise that he was shouting and gesturing at *her*. She tried in vain to open the bedroom window, but it was still stuck fast. Begrudgingly getting out of bed in her lightweight nightdress, Elspeth moved down the length of the boat, trying each window in turn: there was no *way* she was going out on the deck to speak to this rude man in this weather if she could help it. She eventually found that the mechanism on the window in the main saloon was a little looser than the rest; pushing it firmly, it opened a crack and she could *just about* hear the man, who was still shouting and gesturing at her.

The man's image was obscured by the heavy rain, which dripped relentlessly from every part of his outfit. Elspeth couldn't see his face at all; the top half was covered by the low hat, while the bottom half was masked by the stream of rain droplets that were running determinedly from its brim.

"What do you want?" shouted Elspeth through the small, half open window. It wasn't the most polite of greetings, she knew, but the circumstances were not exactly conducive to good manners. She had been woken up after a night of almost no sleep, she was stuck in a little barge in a storm and she could barely see or hear the man due to the terrible weather. Elspeth just wanted him to get straight to the point – whatever that point was – so that she could go back to bed.

The man said something, but his words were half carried away by the noise of the rain.

"What?" yelled Elspeth. "I can't hear you!"

The man tried again, his voice louder this time. "You need to move your boat!" he shouted. "Move it today!"

"I can't!" Elspeth shouted back. She genuinely couldn't. She had no idea how one would even begin to go about such a task. What business was it of his where the boat was? It had been here ever since it officially came into her possession. It wasn't in anyone's way. Why was it a problem?

The man shouted something more, but his words were partly lost in the noise of the torrential rain. Elspeth caught scraps: "Overstay charge", "One hundred and fifty pound fine", "Move down the towpath."

"I can't!" she repeated.

"Why not?" demanded the man through the rain.

"Because I don't know how to drive a boat!" yelled Elspeth in exasperation.

"You can't be serious!" shouted the man. "You're staying on one! That's stupid!"

"It's none of your business! Just leave me alone!" yelled Elspeth, slamming the window shut. Yes, she realised that the man had a point. To move onto a canal boat without any clue how to move it if needed wasn't exactly ideal, but her circumstances *had* been a little extreme. The prospect of living with Janice would lead anybody to make irrational decisions.

Elspeth peeped out of the window, to see that the man was still standing there, utterly drenched, but had appeared to have given up yelling at her. As she watched, he turned away, and seemed to set off down the towpath, presumably to go and shout at somebody else. She was about to retreat back under the covers when she heard a strange noise at the door of the boat; a kind of whimpering. Opening the door with trepidation, Elspeth was surprised to see a very small, very wet, very lovely little dog sitting on the prow. It looked rather sorry for itself, but the moment Elspeth opened the door it brightened, gave a lovely bark of greeting and wagged its tail.

"Oh, you *gorgeous* thing!" exclaimed Elspeth, immediately forgetting about the awful weather and bending down to fuss it. "You need a towel!" She left the door open as she went to fetch one from the bathroom, and the little dog followed her onto *The Blue Belle*, bringing a trail of muddy pawprints in its wake. It seemed grateful for Elspeth's attention, letting her dry its fur off with a towel and lavishing her with licks, friendly little barks and attempts to put its paws on her legs. Lovely as it was to have the little dog on the boat, Elspeth was aware that this clearly wasn't where the dog *should* be. It must have trotted up the gang plank from the towpath; presumably its owners were looking for it. There was nothing else for it; Elspeth would have to brace the weather and go outside with the dog to return it to dry land. Elspeth had no idea where on earth her raincoat would be in all of the boxes, so shrugged on her silky dressing gown as *some* protection against the elements at least, and went out to the prow of the boat. Alas, the shouty man was back. Elspeth heard him before she saw him.

"What on earth are you playing at, moving on to a canal boat with no idea how to move it?" he shouted. "Absolute idiocy!"

He was right, of course. Elspeth had had the very same realisation herself only moments before. But still, it was none of his business. She was about to retort with something of that nature, when the little dog gave a bark of recognition and ran along the gangplank to the man, who acknowledged it with a nod. Elspeth stood for a moment on the prow of *The Blue Belle* watching them, her flimsy dressing gown now utterly soaked through and clinging to her slim frame, as the man looked back towards her. He opened his mouth as if to shout something further, but Elspeth turned on her heel and ducked back into the sanctuary of *The Blue Belle*, slamming the door behind her.

Elspeth realised that she was shaking; partly because of her utter drenching and partly because of the unpleasant, unsettling scene with the man. *What a nasty piece of work*, she thought to herself, as she changed into a dry pair of pyjamas and hung her nightie and dressing gown up to drip dry over the tiny shower. Who did he think he was, waking her up at seven in the morning, shouting at her on her own narrow boat and telling her to move it? Why on earth should she? And who did he think he was? He was probably some middle aged, officious type who had nothing better to do with his time than go round telling other people off, when all *they* were doing was minding their own business and trying to have a lie in. Elspeth made herself a cup of tea and took it back to the safety of her bed. She was exhausted and had been, she had to admit, thoroughly shaken by the storm. She realised that she knew very little about the reality of living on a canal boat and had placed herself in rather a vulnerable position. The man was right about one thing: moving onto a canal boat with no idea how to handle the craft could be dangerous. She resolved to try to get to know some of the other boaters on the canal; perhaps they could give her some advice about how to make this lifestyle work. In the meantime, though, she desperately needed sleep. Finishing her tea, she snuggled back down gratefully under the covers.

It was almost lunchtime when Elspeth re-emerged, her face a little puffy from the combination of under and over-sleeping, but far more refreshed than she had been first thing in the morning. Determined not to be put off her stride by the unreasonable barge man, Elspeth decided that she would spend the afternoon on the next stage of her plan: taking Reggie's clothes to the laundrette to see what could be later donated, then depositing the bags of recyclables and landfill at the local refuse disposal site. It wasn't exactly a glamorous afternoon, but Elspeth knew she'd feel better for having moved her project forwards. In the meantime, though, she needed something to eat. Elspeth had seen a café about a mile down the towpath that seemed to be popular with boaters. She resolved to go there for some brunch and to see if any of the staff or customers could shed any light on the man's rude behaviour this morning.

Ordering scrambled eggs on toast and a cup of tea at the basic but functional café, Elspeth struck up a conversation with the friendly man at the counter. The café wasn't busy, presumably on account of the awful weather that morning, and he seemed happy to talk to her.

"I've just moved onto a canal boat moored about a mile up the towpath," she revealed as they chatted. "I had quite an unpleasant experience this morning, though. Someone came and shouted at me to move the boat. I'm very new to all of this. I don't suppose you have any idea why they might say that?"

The man smiled broadly. "Well, there's all sorts that could be going on there," he said. "Depends on who they were, what type of mooring you're on and how long you've been there."

"Oh. I didn't realise there were different types," Elspeth commented innocently.

The man raised his eyebrows and looked at her askance. "Okay, so you don't know the difference between, say, a waterside mooring, a regular towpath mooring and a mooring at a marina?"

Elspeth shook her head. "Erm, no. Should I?"

"Well, yes. I think you probably should," the man nodded. "Tell you what. We're not that busy this morning. How about I get Cerys to mind the till and I'll take my break now and have a bite to eat with you? I can give you a few pointers."

"I would *really* appreciate that," said Elspeth gratefully. "I'm beginning to realise that I've been quite naïve about this. I just thought you kind of ... parked your boat up wherever you fancied." As she said it, she realised how ridiculous it sounded. Of course you couldn't do that. It would lead to chaos on the waterways. Presumably somebody, somewhere, was managing all of this. *That* hadn't occurred to her before, either.

Eddie, the owner of the café, came over with the scrambled eggs and tea for Elspeth and a coffee and some beans on toast for himself, joining Elspeth at her quiet table. As they enjoyed their brunches, he explained various aspects of life on the canals to

Elspeth: the role of the CRT, the Canals and Rivers Trust, in maintaining and managing the waterways; the standard mooring fee of a little over one hundred pounds a month that Elspeth would need to pay as a boat owner; the understanding that you could only moor for a maximum of fourteen days at a mooring on a towpath; and the availability of Waterside Moorings, managed by the CRT. "So from the sounds of it, you're either on a regular mooring but you've exceeded the fourteen day maximum stay, *or* you have a Waterside Mooring but your contract has run out. Either way, you'll need to do something – either move your boat or renew your contract if you have one, otherwise you *will* get a fine. Sounds like the chap this morning was pretty unpleasant, but he might have a point."

"Oh. I see. I feel a bit of an idiot now," said Elspeth, glumly staring into her tea. She had no idea how to find out what the current state of affairs was, and no money in her budget to pay for an extension to a contract for a Waterside Mooring if, as she suspected, that was what she currently had. "But thank you, Eddie," she said warmly. "That's incredibly helpful."

Finishing her tea and insisting on paying for Eddie's beans on toast and coffee as a thank you, Elspeth made her way back to *The Blue Belle* and got on with her afternoon's tasks. As she sat in the laundrette waiting for Reggie's items to wash in the industrial sized machine, she took out her phone and did a little research. Finding the number of the local CRT mooring manager, she called for some advice, the washing machines chuntering away in the background. Due to her rather embarrassing lack of any paperwork (it was probably in a box somewhere on *The Blue Belle*, but Elspeth currently had no idea where), it took them a while to find her on their records and to verify her story. Once they did, Elspeth was amazed by the news. Yes, they confirmed, *The Blue Belle* was at a residential Waterside Mooring, and the contract had been due for renewal yesterday. Usually, people would communicate their intention to renew in plenty of time before the renewal date, but clearly this hadn't happened. Luckily for Elspeth, no-one else had been waiting for the space, otherwise she might have lost it. As it was, the mooring was available and somebody had renewed it online this morning on Elspeth's behalf, for another six months. Elspeth was speechless.

"But who would do that?" she asked the equally perplexed man on the phone.

"I don't know," he replied. "I can't see much on the system and I probably couldn't give you the information anyway. Maybe you have some sort of guardian angel!"

"Maybe," murmured Elspeth. *Reggie*, she thought to herself. That was the only explanation. Perhaps he had known that the contract would run out soon and had arranged for it to be renewed on his behalf. Maybe he had left instructions with Eliot and Co. She couldn't think of anyone else who would understand the situation or be generous enough to do that for her. Thanking the mooring manager for his time, Elspeth hung up and turned her attention back to Reggie's clothing. Time to move it to the dryer.

Arriving back at *The Blue Belle* three hours later, having stopped off at the refuse disposal site to make a bit of space in her car, Elspeth felt a little more settled as she entered the boat. There would be a lot to learn about life on the canal, and the previous night and day had certainly been a steep learning curve.

Elspeth had popped into a newsagents on her way home to pick up a copy of the popular canal boating magazine *Waterways World*; she figured that if she was going to live on a canal boat, she needed to immerse herself in that way of life and find out as much as she could. Settling herself on the hard, stained sofa in the saloon of *The Blue Belle*, she flicked through the magazine with interest. She was determined to make a go of this, and she resolved to put her upset about the unreasonable, shouty man this morning behind her. Besides, she thought to herself victoriously, he was wrong. She *didn't* need to move her boat. And she *wouldn't* get a fine. Thanks to someone, somewhere, Elspeth was a fully official, paid up resident of her Waterside Mooring. For the next six months, at least.

Chapter 11: Grafting

Clearly, *The Blue Belle* was going to be something of a project. Elspeth could see its potential in her mind's eye: a pretty, calming space just for her; all white stained wooden floors, pastel paint colours and light, pretty fabrics. Unfortunately, the gulf between *The Blue Belle* of her imagination and *The Blue Belle* of her reality was immense.

Elspeth knew that there was no shortcut to achieving her goals for her living space. With an incredibly limited budget which would barely cover materials, let alone labour, Elspeth would be doing most of the work herself, and there was no doubt in her mind that it would be hard graft. She was no stranger to working with fairly heavy duty tools, having learned to use them in her sculptural work, but this would be in a different league. Janice's Rick, himself something of a DIY enthusiast, had agreed to lend Elspeth any tools that she might need, so other than the very specialist equipment that she would rent as and when she needed it, Elspeth's initial outlay would be fairly low. She made a list of all of the work that she planned to do on the narrow boat and drew up a schedule: the rip out would be the first job, and until she began it, she had no way of knowing exactly *how far* she would need to strip the interior back. Once she had taken out everything that would be going, it would be a case of making sure that things were in reasonable order with the electrics and the plumbing on the boat – Elspeth knew that she would need to get professionals in to help her with this. Then, and only then, would the real fun begin:

the fit out. This was the bit that Elspeth was looking forwards to the most: starting to see her vision for the interior come together. Yet, according to her possibly rather optimistic schedule, she wouldn't be at that stage for a couple of months at least.

Donning the white, hooded protective overalls and the dust mask that she had purchased for the task, Elspeth began the rip out with gusto. She would need to transport everything she took out of *The Blue Belle* to the local refuse and recycling centre in her car, and she knew that she would be something of a regular there for the next few weeks. She began with the wooden cladding that covered the walls and ceiling of the narrow boat, realising as she removed the fifth plank and surveyed the hundreds still to go that this would be a significant undertaking. Singing along to her radio, Elspeth worked steadily and methodically along the right side of the boat to begin with, realising as she did so that the insulation would certainly benefit from being replaced. This wasn't a huge surprise: the current insulation would have probably been in situ since Reggie bought the boat. Elspeth got into a rhythm, stripping out a dozen or so planks at a time, then transporting them to the boot of her car with the backseat folded down to give her space, before doing the next section. It was hard graft, but satisfying, and when she stopped for a tea break around mid-morning, she was pleased with her progress.

It was as she sat on the sweet little bench on the prow of *The Blue Belle* that she saw a woman approaching her. At first, she assumed she was just out for walk, but it soon became clear that the woman was making a beeline for her. Elspeth gave her a smile of welcome as she approached the boat.

"Hello," said the woman as she reached the towpath next to *The Blue Belle*. "I thought I'd come over and introduce myself. I'm Mary. Mary Parker. I was a friend of Reggie's."

"Oh! I see!" Of course, Reggie would have got to know people around the places he moored *The Blue Belle*. Elspeth hadn't got her head around the way that the narrow boating community worked yet, but she realised that Reggie wouldn't have lived completely in isolation on the narrow boat.

"Lovely to meet you, Mary," she said. "I'm Elspeth. Would you like to join me for a cup of tea? I've got jammy dodgers."

Mary's face lit up at the mention of jammy dodgers. "Well, I'm on my way to do a bit of shopping, but a tea break would be nice," she said, stepping onto *The Blue Belle* without any further encouragement.

"Come on in while I make the tea if you like," Elspeth offered. "It's a bit of a building site in here, I'm afraid," she continued. "I thought *The Blue Belle* could do with a bit of a makeover, so I'm starting the rip out today." Elspeth and Mary made their way into the galley, where Elspeth found the kettle under its dust sheet. Mary looked around with interest.

"You're right about it needing a makeover," she agreed. "Reggie was brilliant at the maintenance – you won't find a boat of this age in much better condition than *The Blue Belle* – but he wasn't much of a one for interior design."

Elspeth busied herself making Mary's tea. "So how did you know Reggie?" she asked. "It's very strange for me, having inherited *The Blue Belle*. I didn't know Reggie at all; I only met him when I was little," she explained. "I'd really like to find out more about him."

Mary nodded. "Me and Ian, that's my husband, *did* wonder what was going on when you appeared," she said. "Nobody knew who Reggie had left the boat to, and then you showed up in your Fiat Punto!" So, Elspeth thought, my arrival hasn't gone unnoticed.

"I knew Reggie for years," continued Mary as they made their way back onto the prow to sit side by side on the little bench. "Me and Ian have been living on our boat, *The Marian*, for about fifteen years. Met Reggie pretty soon after we moved aboard."

"*The Marian*. That's an interesting name. Why *The Marian*?"

"Mary and Ian. *Marian*. Like those celebrity couple names; you know, Bennifer, or Brangelina."

"Oh!" Elspeth smiled at the idea. "So what was Reggie like?"

Mary sipped her tea thoughtfully. "He lived life on his own terms, I suppose," she said. "A good sort, definitely, but not one for compromise. Him and my Ian always got on like a house on fire. Used to sit up on *The Blue Belle* playing cards for *hours* of an evening. We'll both miss him. So," Mary continued, clearly getting to the point of her visit, "I hope you don't mind me asking, but what's your connection to Reggie? I mean, I know it's none of my business, but, well, Ian and I were a bit curious. We knew Reggie didn't have children – are you a relative of some sort?"

Elspeth shook her head, unsure of how much she should reveal to Mary. She didn't know whether Reggie and Janice's relationship had been common knowledge. She decided that she might as well be honest; as far as she knew, Janice wouldn't mind. "No, we're not related. At first *I* wondered whether we might be! But, no, apparently not. I visited *The Blue Belle* a few times when I was little, with my mum, Janice."

97

Mary's eyes widened. "Janice! Well, I never. You're Janice's girl! We always knew she had a family but I never actually met you. So, after all these years, Janice was still the one for Reggie, eh?" Mary smiled nostalgically. "We had some good times, me, Ian, Janice and Reggie. She's not shy, your mother."

"No, she's not," agreed Elspeth. Janice was many things, but *shy* unfortunately wasn't one of them.

"So what are you going to do with it?" asked Mary, changing the subject. "*The Blue Belle*, I mean?"

"Well, actually, I'm planning to live on it," Elspeth revealed shyly.

"Are you really? Well, Reggie would be delighted, I'm sure. It'll be nice to have a young person around a bit. Me and Ian didn't move onto *The Marian* until we were in our fifties – waited for the children to grow up and move out, then we could do what we wanted! It's quite a transition, though, moving onto a narrow boat. Do you know much about living on the water?"

Elspeth shook her head, glad to have another person to talk to about this. "Nope. Nothing at all. I'm a complete novice. I keep thinking maybe I've taken on too much, but then, well, I don't really have anywhere else to live, so ..."

"*Oh*, it's like that, is it? Well, I'll tell you what, Elspeth, you come to me and Ian with any questions you have. We've been doing this for a long time now, so there's not much about narrow boat living that we can't help you with."

Elspeth smiled gratefully. "Well, actually, there's *already* something I could do with some advice about, Mary. I, um, I don't actually know how to move a narrow boat."

Mary looked at her incredulously. "You *have* driven a narrow boat before, haven't you?" she asked.

Elspeth shook her head. "Actually, no. I don't even know how to switch the engine on."

"Fancy that! Well, you'll definitely need a few pointers. And what about your boat licence? Is that all up to date?

"My boat licence? I didn't know there was such a thing."

Mary chuckled. "And I thought me and Ian were novices when we started on *The Marian*! We've got nothing on *you*. Tell you what, Elspeth. I know Reggie will've kept the engine in pretty good order. How about we switch her on now for ten minutes and I'll give you a few pointers to get you started?"

"That would be such a relief!" exclaimed Elspeth, running inside to get the keys.

Mary showed Elspeth how to insert the key and turn it to the position marked 'heat'. After waiting a few minutes for the indicator lights to come on, they turned it to the 'start' position. Elspeth sensed a little thrill run through her as she felt *The Blue Belle's* engine running for the first time; it was like the boat was coming back to life. Elspeth had no intention of actually moving the boat anywhere that day, so Mary simply showed Elspeth the three positions of the gear lever: neutral, forward and reverse, and explained how to work the tiller. "Obviously you'll need some practice," said Mary, "and there are courses you can do to help you learn, but those are the basics. And at least you know she works!" she said, switching of the engine after it had been running for a while.

"Thank you so much, Mary!" Elspeth enthused. "That makes me feel so much better. And I'll find out about the boat license you mentioned. Gosh, there's more to this lifestyle than I realised!"

Mary smiled and gestured to the interior of *The Blue Belle*. "And what about the work? You're not planning on doing that all by yourself, are you?"

Elspeth nodded slowly. "Yes," she said. "That's the idea. Although I know I'll need to get trades in at some point; I can't manage electrics or anything to do with the engine myself."

"I'll put you in touch with my Stephen for when you're at that point," offered Mary. "He's an electrician. He's about your age. He can come and give you a hand."

"That would be amazing!" smiled Elspeth. "If he wouldn't mind."

Mary grinned and gave her a wink. "He'll do as his mother tells him," she said. "Right, I'd better be off. Want to get to Lidl and back before lunch. Good to meet you, Elspeth."

"You too, Mary," returned Elspeth warmly, grateful to have made a connection with the narrow boat community and to know that *The Blue Belle* was in decent working order.

Re-energised by her conversation, Elspeth returned to the rip-out with renewed energy. The possibility of help with the electrics from Mary's son Stephen sounded promising; Elspeth hadn't been sure where to start in terms of looking for tradespeople. Humming contentedly along to the radio, Elspeth fell back into the rhythm of stripping out the cladding, and by the time she stopped for lunch she had nearly completed a whole wall. She decided that the afternoon would be best spent doing a trip to the refuse centre then cleaning up as best she could so that it would be possible to sleep on *The Blue Belle* that night.

It was as Elspeth took out the old strips of cladding from the boat, clearing areas of rubbish as she went, that she made her discovery. Stooping to gather up a pile of the old bits of wood from the floor, Elspeth noticed a metal box wedged next to the water tank. She hadn't seen in before, what with all of the dirty washing and general detritus on the boat when she started the work. Intrigued, she picked it up and opened it. It was around thirty by twenty centimetres in size, with no lock or any markers on it to suggest what it might hold. Peeping inside, Elspeth realised that she had found something important: this was Reggie's special box.

Elspeth knew that lots of people had a special box. She had one herself ... hidden *somewhere* in all of her currently unpacked belongings. It was the box where you would keep the bits and bobs that were important to you in some way; useful or sentimental, perhaps. Reggie's box was filled with a few small metal plaques, presumably souvenirs from places that he had travelled to on *The Blue Belle*, plus some old photographs. Elspeth was astonished, and somewhat delighted, to find a couple of pictures of Reggie with Janice, clearly taken on sunny, summer days when they had spent time together on *The Blue Belle*. There were a few old coins too; that didn't surprise Elspeth in the slightest: for some reason she imagined Reggie was the kind of person who'd be interested in that sort of thing. Then there was an envelope. Picking it up and turning it over, Elspeth was surprised to see her own name staring back at her, in spidery, uncertain handwriting. Her eyes wide, Elspeth gently opened the envelope to find a brief letter inside:

Dear Elspeth,

Now, I'm not much of a one for writing, but I thought this was important. I've seen a solicitor today – a bloke called Henry. Nice enough bloke, but a bit wet. Told him I want to leave 'The Blue Belle' to you. He's going to see to all the paperwork and such like. Now, I don't know how long I have, but I don't think it's long. Never wanted to think about all that business, but seems like I have to now. And 'The Blue Belle', she's the main thing I'll leave behind. No children, no wife, no house. Just a narrow boat. Well, I say just, but that doesn't do her justice. I'm proud of her. She's my legacy, for want of a better word. And I want you to have her.

Now, I know I don't know you. Not really. But I feel like I've watched you grow up. Janice talks about you all the time. She's not the easiest of women – nobody knows that better than me – but she loves you, in her way. And she's proud of you. But she's worried about you. She doesn't rate that Peter you're with. Sounds like you need to ditch him for starters. And sounds to me like you're creative. You need to follow your own path, Elspeth. Nothing like the freedom of living on the water for that. I knew it when I met you when you were little. You loved it on here! Mucking about with the tiller, poking around in the galley, wanting to find out where the engine was. You and that boy playing hide and seek in the saloon. You were at home on here. And it brought 'The Blue Belle' to life when you came aboard.

I've not told Janice what I've done. We've not seen each other much over the last few years. Think she's got a new bloke. Well, fair play to her. I wasn't ever much of a boyfriend for her. Couldn't give her whatever it was she wanted. She wants a lot, your mother.

So 'The Blue Belle' is yours, Elspeth. I hope you still like her and she still likes you. She's in pretty good nick – you'll probably want to freshen her up a bit, make her a bit more homely and all. Sorry about the mess. I've never been much of a one for clearing up and these days I just can't be bothered. Privilege of being a grumpy old man. Nobody else's business.

Enjoy her, Elspeth. And give her a bit of love.

Yours,
Reginald Blackwater (Esq)

Elspeth read the letter twice, her eyes filling with tears. She already felt that she knew Reggie a little, from the flashes of her childhood memories, from the presence she still felt a little on *The Blue Belle*. And here he was, writing directly to her. Elspeth pressed the letter to her heart; she somehow felt a connection to this self-named *grumpy old man*. And he said that Janice had talked about her to him! How strange. She always imagined that Janice was rather disinterested in her. Elspeth looked again at the photographs of Janice and Reggie: in them, Janice looked as happy as Elspeth had ever seen her. And Reggie, with his tanned face, his broad shoulders, his tattooed arms and his broad grin (which Elspeth couldn't help notice was missing a couple of teeth) looked like someone Elspeth would have been interested to get to know. She resolved to give the photos to Janice and see whether she would like the old coins as well; knowing Janice, she'd try to find out whether they were worth anything.

Putting everything safely back in the box for now, Elspeth continued the task of transporting the old cladding to her car. She had a new phrase in her mind now for the work that she was doing on *The Blue Belle*, and it bathed the arduous, tedious task in a rosy glow. In accordance with Reggie's wishes, Elspeth wouldn't just restore *The Blue Belle*; she would give her a bit of love.

Chapter 12: Hapless Henry

It had been a physically draining day on *The Blue Belle*. Having removed all of the sauna-like cladding from the interior the previous week, Elspeth had spent the last three days on the quite frankly unpleasant job of taking out the old insulation. Wearing a respirator mask and protective clothing all day left her feeling itchy and claustrophobic, and she was glad to call it a day at 5.30pm, when she returned from her second trip to the tip. She had by now removed almost all of the old insulation from *The Blue Belle*, and would spend the next day preparing the walls for the new insulation which would be delivered in stages next week. Thankfully, the boat's shell was in remarkably good condition. There were no leaks or particularly problematic rust patches, so she could move to the next step without any major remedial work, which was great news. Elspeth showered off the dust from her day's labours before contemplating what to do with herself for the evening. It was a Wednesday, and she knew that her friends were rarely up for a mid-week night out these days. Yet she didn't feel like another night in on *The Blue Belle* in its current state. The walls were essentially stripped back to the metal shell and the boat didn't feel particularly welcoming. Despite her tight budget, Elspeth decided to treat herself to a meal at the pretty pub a little further up the towpath, *The Swan*. She had been there a few times already and was on nodding terms with some of the locals. She could take a book, settle down in a corner and while away a couple of cosy hours.

Donning jeans and a fresh t-shirt, Elspeth felt like a million dollars after her day in the uncomfortable protective boiler suit. A spring in her step at the thought of a delicious home cooked pie at the pub, she slung her bag over her shoulder, locked the door of *The Blue Belle* and set off up the towpath. It was a beautiful evening, and Elspeth paused to appreciate the gold and blue of the early evening sky and the peaceful, still water of the canal. She said a silent thank you to Reggie for giving her this gift; it was truly a special way to live.

The pub wasn't particularly busy when Elspeth entered, and she was able to choose a seat in her favourite corner. Sipping a soft drink as she perused the menu, pretending to herself that she *might* order a salad while secretly knowing full well it would be the pie with chips, she said hello to a few faces she recognised and privately congratulated herself on slowly becoming part of the community. After ordering her food, which unsurprisingly *wasn't* the salad, she settled into her book, a 1930s murder mystery in which she was fairly confident that she had already worked out who the murderer was. Her attention was pulled away from her novel by a commotion at the table next to hers.

"You *idiot*! That's gone all over my new dress!" a young woman shrieked, standing up quickly and shaking out the fabric of the pretty, short sleeved floral outfit she was wearing. "You're *so* clumsy, Henry! Being out with you is just ... *embarrassing*!"

"Oh, no! I'm sorry? It's these new contact lenses; I'm just not used to them yet? Please, Amy, sit down and we can ask for a napkin?"

"No, Henry! I am *not* sitting down. I am *so* fed up of this. I don't even know why I'm bothering to try and date you. I wasn't going to say anything this evening; I was going to give things one more try, but that is *it*! There's no future in this, Henry. No future at all." The woman calmed down slightly after her outburst and her tone softened. "Look, you're nice and everything, don't get me wrong. But I need a *real* man, you know? Someone who can take the lead a bit. Someone who I can rely on. And someone who doesn't make everything sound like a question! I'm sorry, Henry. It's over." And with that, the young woman walked out of the pub, leaving little puddles of white wine on the table and the chair where she had been sitting.

The mini-scene had been observed by a few of the pub's customers, who now discretely turned their attention back to their own business. Elspeth did the same, resting her eyes on her book and attempting to read, yet she couldn't help but feel that the man was familiar from somewhere. Glancing at him furtively as he stared disconsolately into his pint of bitter, she tried to place him. He was certainly attractive, with pale blue eyes, dark hair and kind features. She liked the way he was dressed, a pale blue shirt complementing his eyes. Elspeth realised it was his voice she recognised more than his face. That rising intonation. The woman had called him Henry. Of course! *Eliot and Co*. He looked very different out of work: gone were the badly fitting suit, the thick glasses and the pile of manila files. She wouldn't have even recognised him had she not heard him speak.

Elspeth hesitated for a few moments. Henry didn't seem to be in a rush to leave the pub; if anything, the rather public dumping seemed to have glued him to his seat. Elspeth wondered how she would feel in his situation: would she want to just be left to herself, or would she appreciate a friendly ear? It was a tricky one, but she decided to try the latter. If Henry seemed uncomfortable, she could just say a polite hello, then return to her own table. She stood up and took a couple of steps towards him.

"Henry?" He looked up, clearly unable to place her for a moment.

"Yes? Oh! You're the girl with the barge?"

"That's right. Elspeth. Hello again. Do you mind if I join you for a moment?"

"Please do," Henry said, gesturing to the seat opposite him. "Although it might be a bit wet?"

Elspeth nodded and took a pile of napkins from the centre of the table to make a little cushion. "There," she said, settling herself in. "That's not too bad. A bit damp, but fine ... I, um, I couldn't help seeing what just happened."

Henry shook his head glumly. "I don't blame Amy," he said, his high rise intonation momentarily deserting him. "I'm a terrible date. I'm so clumsy and I never know what I'm supposed to do, you know? These new contact lenses don't help." He gestured towards his eyes. "I thought, you know, they'd be better than the glasses? But they're really irritating? And I'm not used to judging distances with them yet. Hence knocking over her wine?"

Elspeth nodded. Perhaps it was an effect of the high rise intonation, or perhaps it was the fact that she had just watched him get dumped: either way, she had an overwhelming desire to reassure Henry; to comfort him and to make him feel better about himself.

"Well, maybe it just wasn't meant to be," Elspeth said soothingly. "Sometimes, even if we really like somebody and they really like us, it doesn't necessarily mean it will work as a relationship."

Henry lifted his gaze from his pint. "Maybe you're right," he said. "I *did* really like her. And I think she really did like me? In some ways? But like you say, that doesn't mean we were necessarily right for each other."

Elspeth nodded. "I had a break up recently, actually," she confided. "It was quite a big one, I suppose. We'd been together for three years. We were living together and we were engaged."

"Oh gosh!" exclaimed Henry. "That *is* a big one. You think you're going to marry someone and then you're not? What happened?"

"Well, it turns out that he had feelings for someone else," Elspeth said simply. She decided not to go into the whole Peter buying his own engagement ring and her catching him with Maria debacle; it was water under the bridge now. Elspeth focused on what she thought was the most important part. "The thing is, after it happened, I realised it was absolutely for the best. Peter – my ex – wasn't right for me at all. And *I* wasn't right for *him*. We just didn't make each other as happy as we could be. And splitting up with him meant that I had to make some changes in my life. It was around the same time as I inherited *The Blue Belle* from Reggie; it gave me the push to take a different path."

"So what are you doing with the boat?" asked Henry. "I must say, it was one of the more unusual bequests I've had to deal with?"

"I'm living on it," announced Elspeth with a smile. "It needs a lot of work, so I'm doing that step by step myself, and in the meantime I'm ... well, I'm living on a barge-cum-building-site. That's why I came here for dinner tonight, actually. The inside of the boat is pretty much stripped back to metal at the moment, so it doesn't exactly feel very cosy!"

"Wow, Elspeth. That's so inspiring? You're doing it yourself? I wouldn't know where to start with something like that. I'm fine with files and contracts, but I'm not much of a one for practical things? How do you know what to do?"

Elspeth shrugged. "I don't always," she smiled. "But I trained as a sculptural artist, so I'm used to working with materials, and I *do* have a vision for what I'm trying to achieve. I guess the rest of it I just figure out as I go along ... with the help of lots of how-to videos!"

Henry was clearly genuinely impressed. By this time, Elspeth's delicious looking pie and chips had arrived and Henry eyed it covetously. "I think I might treat myself to one of those?" he said. "I'll go and ask at the bar. And," he said shyly, "would it be alright if I bought you a drink?"

Elspeth felt a little flutter of excitement. It was a long time since she'd had a drink with a man other than Peter. She realised that this wasn't a date – if anything, she was simply standing in for Henry's *real* date who had left after the wine spillage episode – but it felt nice nonetheless. "I'd love a drink," she said honestly. "Maybe a dry white wine?"

Henry beamed and seemed to puff out his chest a little at her acceptance. "I'll be right back," he said, without a trace of high rise intonation.

Elspeth sat back contently in the still rather damp chair as she tucked into her dinner and watched Henry ordering at the bar. He was clearly intelligent, and, without the thick glasses and the terrible suit, really quite attractive. Yes, he seemed a slightly unsure of himself, and his conversational tone was a little annoying, but he could perhaps be trained out of that ... Elspeth found herself wondering whether Amy's loss that evening might be her gain.

Somehow, Elspeth's glass of white wine turned into two, and she and Henry had an utterly delightful and mutually therapeutic evening. He told her a little more about his, now apparently finished, relationship with Amy; about his job at Eliot and Co.; about his rather domineering mother; about the little flat he had bought a year ago and felt constantly anxious about because it was in an old building and needed maintenance that he really didn't know how to carry out. Elspeth told him about her recent departure from working as a paralegal; about her feeling that she wanted to find a different path and that living on *The Blue Belle* would somehow help her; about her frustrating relationship with Janice. It was altogether a lovely evening; Elspeth felt that she had found somebody she could talk to and perhaps connect with. She found herself disappointed when the pub called last orders and their evening was over.

As they left the pub, Henry nodded towards the towpath. "Can I walk you back to *The Blue Belle*?" he asked.

"Thank you, Henry, but no, I'll be fine."

"Well, if you're sure? And, I'm really glad that I met you tonight, Elspeth. It turned a bad evening into a very good one? I hope you don't mind suggesting it, but, would you like to meet for a drink again sometime?"

"I think I'd like that," replied Elspeth. "Thank you, Henry." They exchanged numbers and Elspeth walked back along the towpath to *The Blue Belle*, a warm feeling inside her and a spring in her step. She wasn't necessarily on the *lookout* for a new relationship, but she was certainly open to possibilities. She couldn't help but feel that her chance meeting with Henry tonight was one such prospect.

Chapter 13: Community

The small fund for *The Blue Belle* that Reggie had left Elspeth – all one hundred and fifty five pounds and eighty-two pence of it - had been spent weeks ago, and Elspeth's small savings pot had been exhausted by the cost of the boat's survey and the protective suit and equipment she had needed to buy for the rip out of *The Blue Belle*'s interior. Elspeth knew that it wouldn't be long until she would need to spend some *real* money on the narrowboat: there would be insulation, plaster board, paint, fabrics, and she didn't even want to *think* about the cost of hiring tradespeople to do the jobs she didn't have the skills to do herself. She thought back to Mary's mention of her son, Stephen. She should really contact him to find out whether he'd be willing to give her a favourable quotation for the electrical work and maybe take a look over the engine bay for her. Mary had popped in a few times since her initial visit and had left Stephen's contact details; Elspeth made a mental note to call the number Mary had scribbled down for her over the next few days.

However she looked at it, one thing was certain: Elspeth needed to get a job. And fast. Ideally one where they paid weekly or fortnightly; she wasn't sure that she could even get to the end of the month without maxing out her overdraft again. The trouble was, Elspeth really didn't know where to start. She didn't want to look for another paralegal role; she agreed with Nina that she wasn't a good fit for that world and, besides, she needed a job that she could work around her restoration of *The Blue Belle*. Working an office job from nine-to-five every day wouldn't leave her much time or energy to tackle her enormous project. Plus, Elspeth reasoned that she didn't need a particularly high wage now that her living costs were so low – no rent to pay and minimal utilities – but more a steady trickle of income to allow her to buy materials as needed for the re-fit of *The Blue Belle* and to support her simple lifestyle.

Setting off on a mid-morning walk along the canal for a well-earned break from her current restoration task of sanding down the wooden kitchen door fronts, which she intended to repaint and reuse, Elspeth enjoyed the fresh air and the feeling of the warm sunshine on her back as she watched the light sparkle on the surface of the canal. She had decided to wend her steps towards a sweet little café she had passed a few times but never visited, around a mile and a half up the towpath, where she intended to treat herself to the cheapest hot drink they offered. As she approached the café, *The Waterside*, she noticed with pleasurable anticipation that there were currently a couple of outdoor wooden tables available, and resolved to enjoy her drink at one of them once she had ordered inside. As she passed the window of the café, Elspeth saw an A5 card sellotaped to the window, with a message scrawled on it in black felt-tip pen. "Help wanted. Part-time. <u>Must</u> be able to work lunchtimes. Experience working with customers and with food desirable. Enquire within." Elspeth surveyed the delightful café, with its blackboard announcing today's bakes and a special offer on cream teas. In that moment, all of her worries about what she should do for work evaporated. She realised that something like this would be perfect. It would provide her with a small but regular income, give her ample time to work on *The Blue Belle*, *and* have the advantage of helping

114

her to integrate a little more into the local community. Elspeth knew that she didn't have as much experience as the café might be hoping for, but she had *some*. And if anyone understood the charm and appeal of a pretty café and a slice of cake, it was Elspeth. She approached the counter and was greeted by a rather pink-cheeked woman in her fifties, whose unruly hair seemed determined to escape from the hat she was wearing to cover it.

"What can I get you, love?" she asked.

"Well, I came in for a cup of tea," Elspeth began, "but then I saw your sign – you know, help wanted? And I wondered whether I might be able to apply for the job."

"Oh! Right. Yes, we do still need somebody. We've had a couple in asking already but none of them wants to work the lunchtimes and that's our busiest part of the day. Tell you what, let me get you your tea then when it's quiet I'll pop out with an application form and tell you a bit more about it."

"Thanks. That would be great," Elspeth smiled, immediately taking a liking to the woman. She paid for her tea, then took it outside to drink in the sunshine. The woman joined her after about five minutes.

"Right then. I'm Anna, by the way. And you are?"

"Elspeth. Elspeth Henley."

"Right, Elspeth. Here's an application form. Just the usual things – you know, name, address, relevant experience and all that. But we might as well have an informal chat about it while you're here. Why do you want the job?"

"Well, I'm looking for something part time because I'm working on restoring a canal boat. So I'm pretty flexible with the hours I can do, it's just that I don't want a full nine-to-five. And something like this would be perfect," Elspeth continued. "I love baking; I mean, I'm guessing the job's probably more front of house, but I'm confident with baking and food prep too, plus I have a little experience waiting tables from when I was a student. And your café's delightful," Elspeth added honestly. "I just think it would be a nice place to work."

Anna gave her a broad smile. "So which boat's yours?" she asked, nodding towards the canal.

"*The Blue Belle*," Elspeth revealed. "Do you know it?"

Anna's face registered recognition. "Yes, I know the one! Didn't an older gentleman used to own it? What was his name ... Roger?"

"Reggie," suppled Elspeth. "Yes, he did. He passed away a few months ago and he left it to me in his will. It was all quite a surprise. So, to cut a long story short, I've moved onto the boat while I'm restoring it, and I left my last job several weeks ago, so something like this would be ideal."

Anna beamed. "It certainly would. Look, I'll tell you what, Elspeth. Obviously we'll need you to fill in the form so we can check everything stacks up, but it seems to me like you'd fit in perfectly here. And you bake as well, you say?"

"Yes. Mostly just for friends so far, but they seem to like what I make!"

"What's your favourite recipe?"

"Oh, chocolate brownies. Obviously. But I also make really good, chewy cookies and a very light Victoria Sponge."

"Wow. You had me at chocolate brownies. We're mostly looking for someone to take orders, run the till and clear away, but if you could rustle up a few baked goods now and again that would be a bonus, particularly on the days when me or Anita has a day off. Hypothetically, when could you start, Elspeth?"

"Tomorrow?" said Elspeth with a grin.

"Love the enthusiasm, Elspeth. Tomorrow might be a bit of a push to get you officially on the books, but how about your bring me the application form tomorrow and, if everything looks tickety-boo, we'll get you started next week?"

Elspeth nodded. "That would be amazing! Thanks Anna. I'll get this back to you first thing in the morning."

"Great. I'll leave you to your tea for now – might as well enjoy the perks of still being a customer!" Anna laughed.

Elspeth did indeed enjoy her tea. She people-watched as she sat at the simple wooden outdoor table, noticing the rhythms of the café; the way that there seemed to be a steady stream of walkers popping in and out of the small building, some stopping, like her, to enjoy their cakes and beverages at the outdoor tables, others continuing their walk with a takeaway coffee or maybe an ice-cream on this sunny day. She could see why the café was advertising for another member of staff: poor Anna was rushed off her feet, trying to simultaneously staff the indoor counter, bring out hot orders and clear the tables. Elspeth was almost tempted to give her a hand regardless of whether she was currently employed by the café or not, but realised she really *should* use her day to make more progress on the kitchen units. Making sure to take her own cup back inside to save Anna another trip, Elspeth made her way back to *The Blue Belle* feeling refreshed and positive; if her application for a job at *The Waterside* were successful, she felt that it would help this new chapter in her life to take a clearer shape; she would have a structure to her days beyond her self-imposed work-schedule on *The Blue Belle*, and she would have social interaction outside of her immediate small circle of friends and family.

That evening, five kitchen cupboard doors thoroughly sanded and prepped, Elspeth settled down in her bed at the back of the narrowboat to fill out her application form. It was currently the only space on the narrow boat that was in any way conducive to relaxation – the galley kitchen and the main saloon were currently in total disarray, with power tools filling the floor space, no doors on the kitchen cupboards and the walls of the boat awaiting their insulation and plasterboard. Elspeth had also hired a floor sander so that she could make a start on the wooden floors of *The Blue Belle* the next week, and this took up a significant amount of room in the living area of the boat. Elspeth was grateful it was summer, so at least she could open some of the windows on *The Blue Belle* and get a bit of fresh air circulating. Propped up again some pillows on her bed, Elspeth worked through the application form for the café carefully and neatly, presenting her previous experience of waiting tables in a somewhat flattering light in order to make herself sound like an appealing candidate. She realised that she wanted this job more than she had ever wanted her paralegal role. That had felt like something she *should* do. This was something she *wanted* to do.

As promised, Elspeth took the application form back to *The Waterside* the next morning just after they opened at eight-thirty. Anna greeted her warmly and introduced her to the other staff at the café: Anna's husband John, who looked after the upkeep of the premises and did most of the ordering and accounts, Anita who did most of the baking and Tanya who, like Elspeth, was part-time and tended to cover weekends and busier periods to give Anna, John and Anita alternate time off. The café opened seven days a week, so it was clearly a big commitment for Anna and John. Anna all but assured Elspeth that the job was hers, promising to look over her application form whenever she got a minute that day and to call her that evening. While she was there, Elspeth decided to sample one of *The Waterside's* breakfast muffins – it was delicious, and Elspeth was glad that she had a day's physical work ahead of her to balance out the slight overindulgence.

Arriving back at *The Blue Belle*, Elspeth got straight to work on her job for that day: painting the kitchen units that she had prepped the day before. She was planning to paint them a simple, fresh white and to add pretty shabby chic handles in a pale green, which she had already sourced from a vintage shop. The worktop itself would be sanded back and oiled rather than painted. Elspeth was confident that the eventual effect would be stylish and pretty. As Elspeth worked, singing along to the radio, she realised that this was the part of the restoration she enjoyed the most: the glide of her paintbrush along the smooth wood was immensely satisfying, and she could begin to imagine how the simple kitchen units would look. Most of the decoration of the narrow boat would have to wait until some more of the bigger jobs had been done: Elspeth knew that she should get an electrician in before she tackled the insulation, as it would be irritating to have to undo any work she had already done if there were any problems. She remembered the phone number Mary had given her and decided to give Stephen a call when she had a break for lunch.

Sitting on the prow of *The Blue Belle* a few hours later, with half of the kitchen doors painted and drying in the sunshine on the small deck of the boat, she finished her cheese sandwich and pulled out her mobile to try Mary's son. Elspeth had been expecting it to go to voicemail and was surprised when a friendly sounding voice answered.

"Hello?"

"Hi Stephen. My name's Elspeth. I got your number from your mum, Mary."

"Elspeth! Yes, mum said you might call. I hear you're working on Reggie's old boat."

"Yes!" Elspeth was flattered that Mary had thought to mention her and that Stephen had remembered who she was.

"So, do you want me to come and have a look over it with you?" asked Stephen amiably. "I love working with canal boats. Mum and Dad's one, *The Marian*, is a pretty similar age to *The Blue Belle* so I've got a fair idea of what you'll be dealing with."

"That would be great, thanks Stephen. When would you be able to come and have a look?"

"I'll be finished today's jobs around four. How about I pop over then and have a nosey?"

Elspeth's face lit up. She had expected she'd have to wait far longer for Stephen's expertise. "Fantastic. I'd appreciate that, Stephen. Do you know where to find me?"

"Of course. You're not far up the towpath from mum and dad. See you later, Elspeth."

Elspeth found that she had a smile on her face when she hung up the phone. Stephen had a genial air about him, on the phone at least. He sounded warm and friendly. Elspeth thought for a moment; Mary seemed to be a similar age to Janice ... she had mentioned that Stephen was a similar age to *her* ...

120

Elspeth smiled and shook her head at her presumptuousness. Of course, it didn't *matter* what age Stephen was; he was simply coming to give her a quotation for any electrical work that *The Blue Belle* might need. Yet he *had* sounded really nice over the phone ... Treating herself to a cookie for energy before getting back to the kitchen cupboards, Elspeth found that she was quite looking forwards to seeing what – or who – four o'clock would bring.

Chapter 14: You Need A Stephen

Cupboard painting completed, Elspeth put the kettle on as the time approached four o'clock. She felt inexplicably nervous. *He's just coming to see to the electrics*, she reminded herself. Keeping half an eye on the towpath as she pottered around inside *The Blue Belle*, Elspeth was excited to see a fair-haired, broad shouldered young man of around her age approaching the boat, wearing black work trousers and a navy t-shirt embossed with a logo. He was carrying a heavy toolbox as if it weighed nothing. Elspeth was in no doubt that *this* was Stephen.

"Elspeth!' he greeted her as if she were an old friend. "Great job you're doing on here." Stephen nodded at the cupboard doors drying outside and the general evidence of ongoing work on the canal boat. "I mean, Reggie was always one to look after the practical side of things on here, but this girl has been in need of an upgrade for a while. You doing the work yourself?"

"As much as I can," said Elspeth, suddenly shy. "There are a few jobs that I know I don't have the skillset for, though. Like the electrics."

"Well, good job I'm here then, isn't it? You need a Stephen." He smiled broadly at Elspeth, his green eyes crinkling slightly at the corners, and she couldn't help but feel that perhaps she *did* need a Stephen, in more ways than one.

"Can I get you a cup of tea? Or coffee?" she offered.

"Tea would be great. Two sugars please," said Stephen, setting down his tool box. "Right, shall I have a look around?"

Stephen spent the next hour or so tinkering around with the fuse-box, storage batteries and various wires on *The Blue Belle*, all the while keeping up a lively, amiable conversation with Elspeth. It appeared that Stephen was very open about ... well, most things ... and by the time he had finished his initial inspection of the boat's electrics, Elspeth knew about everything ranging from his most recent girlfriend (they had broken up two months' previously because she was too clingy), his relationship with his mum and dad (brilliant people but they needed to stop worrying about him) and the reasons he had chosen to become an electrician (always wanted to do something practical, not a fan of all of that reading and writing nonsense). He asked questions too, and Elspeth found herself telling him about her breakup with Peter Penguin, her difficulties with Janice and her recent application for a job at *The Waterside* after her unsuccessful attempts at being a sculptural artist and a paralegal. Elspeth almost felt like they had been on a first date, but rather than a candlelit dinner, the setting had been an electrical inspection of a narrow boat.

His inspection completed, Stephen and Elspeth went to sit on the deck of *The Blue Belle* with another cup of tea while he talked her through his recommendations. Elspeth was delighted to hear that the electrics on the boat were in pretty good shape. Elspeth learned that Stephen was a trained marine electrician, as the electrical installations on boats had some differences to those on land. He explained to her that *The Blue Belle* would draw power from batteries when it was cruising, but would use power from a marina or waterside mooring where available. Essentially, everything was in safe, working order.

Stephen suggested that Elspeth would probably need to install a new fuse box in the near future simply due to the age of the old one, but it was currently working fine. As for the wiring, there were a couple of areas that would benefit from an upgrade before she did the fit out, but nothing major. Elspeth was relieved.

"And roughly how much are we talking, Stephen?" she asked. "I'm guessing this kind of thing is relatively expensive."

Stephen made a so-so face. "Well, obviously there's the cost of the materials, but it shouldn't be more than a hundred quid or so."

Elspeth nodded. "And the labour?"

Stephen gave her a cheeky grin. "You don't think I'm going to charge *you* for labour, do you? I mean, firstly, mum would have a *right* go at me, and secondly, I quite like the idea of coming and giving you a hand with things on *The Blue Belle*. I could help you a bit with the engine bay as well if you like? No charge or anything, just a bit of a project and we could hang out."

"Oh! Well, that's .. very generous of you," returned Elspeth, wondering whether she should clarify exactly what Stephen's expectations were. Was this a favour to his mum as Mary and Elspeth were practically neighbours on the towpath? Was it simply a friendly gesture from someone who quite enjoyed tinkering around on canal boats? Or did Stephen have any designs on her? Elspeth wondered briefly whether she should find an opportunity to mention her upcoming drink with Henry, which they had arranged for later that week, but reasoned that she and Henry weren't exactly *dating* as such, and besides, it might seem presumptuous of her to assume that Stephen would even care.

They arranged for Stephen to come over the next Thursday with the materials and make a start on the work. Elspeth was grateful; it meant that she would finally be able to start re-fitting the boat. Stephen looked at his watch; it was almost seven. Elspeth realised he had been there for the best part of three hours and it had flown by. He really was good company.

"Right. Well, I'd best be off and get some dinner. Tell you what, Elspeth. Do you have any plans this evening?"

Elspeth shook her head. "Not unless you count sitting in a floating building site with a book," she said with a smile.

"How's about it then? Come to the pub with me; my treat. I landed a big job today to do the electrical work on a new estate they're building. I'll be flush for the next few months. It'd be nice to celebrate."

Elspeth hesitated. What was this? A mate's drink or a date? Stephen was so confident and so casual that it was hard to tell. If it was a mate thing, she was definitely *in*. Stephen was interesting, easy to talk to, and, Elspeth could tell, a good laugh. But if it was a date thing ... Elspeth wasn't sure. Stephen was certainly attractive, but he absolutely wasn't Elspeth's usual type. She reflected that he would be far more the kind of man Minnie would go for: practical, no-nonsense, good fun. But then, Elspeth thought, her own previous choices in men hadn't *exactly* worked out very well. The free-spirited creatives she had dated in her early twenties had been wonderful company but utterly unreliable, while Peter had been sensible to the point of lacking emotional intelligence. Maybe she should just be open to seeing where things went with Stephen. One thing was certain: he clearly didn't overthink things the way Elspeth sometimes did. Plus, she realised, a night at the pub with Stephen was infinitely preferable to another night on her building site, where she would quite literally be watching paint dry on the kitchen cupboards.

"Alright," she agreed. "I'd like that. Do you need to go and change or anything?" Elspeth nodded to his work trousers.

"Nah. It's not posh or anything. These'll be fine. Shall we?"

"Yes! Why not? I'll just get my bag." And with that, Elspeth and Stephen set off along the towpath together in the direction of a pub in the town. Elspeth was quite glad that he hadn't suggested *The Swan*, the canal side pub she'd been at the other night with Henry. Of course, she reminded herself, she and Henry *weren't* officially dating and this *wasn't* a date with Stephen, but still, she would have felt a bit odd sitting at a table for two in the same pub but with a different man in the space of a fortnight.

Stephen chose a lively pub in town where he seemed to know almost everyone; he was clearly a gregarious sort, and Elspeth found herself experiencing an entirely different evening than she would have had with Peter or with Henry. They sat on high stools at a small table near the bar, and Stephen ordered the fish and chips while Elspeth went for a simple pasta dish. They had plenty to talk about; Stephen was interested in her work on *The Blue Belle*, and seemed genuinely impressed by her practical skills. She explained that she had learned how to handle several of the more heavy duty tools in her training as a sculptural artist.

"I would never have thought that," Stephen commented. "Always thought you artistic types were just messing around with paint brushes or something. Didn't realise there was anything useful to it."

Elspeth chose not to engage with Stephen's rather limited and disparaging view of artists, realising that many of her friends at art school would quite possibly have been similarly dismissive about electricians. Instead, she took the complement as she thought it was intended, and felt proud of what she had achieved so far on *The Blue Belle*. The evening passed quickly, and before Elspeth knew it, she had enjoyed three glasses of mediocre wine and the bar staff were turning the lights on to encourage people out of the pub. Elspeth was still unsure about what exactly the evening had been; despite Stephen's many friends and acquaintances in the pub, it had very much been just the two of them for most of the evening and they had enjoyed easy, open conversation. Elspeth knew from experience that the moment when they would go their separate ways might be a telling point. Obviously Stephen would be seeing her soon to do the electrical work on the boat, but would he suggest seeing her again as a date? Elspeth was unsure of what *she* wanted, or whether she should suggest anything herself. Stephen was clearly an attractive possibility, but she had left things open with Henry, and after the way that things had ended with Peter, Elspeth didn't want to jump into anything unless she was sure.

It was a lovely night, the air still fairly warm even as they left the pub after closing time.

"Let me walk you back to *The Blue Belle*," said Stephen amiably. "Mum and Dad'll probably still be up on *The Marian*; I'll pop in and say hello before I go home."

Elspeth agreed, glad to have Stephen's company for the walk back to her boat. As they arrived at *The*

Blue Belle, Stephen paused and slipped his arm around Elspeth's waist. "I've had a great time tonight, Elspeth," he murmured, moving closer to her. "How about a kiss to end a lovely evening?"

Elspeth found herself relieved at his directness. "I think I'd like that," she said honestly, turning herself to face him.

It was the first kiss Elspeth had experienced since splitting up with Peter, and, she had to admit, *their* relationship hadn't exactly been a passionate one. Locked in an embrace with Stephen, the air rustling in the trees that lined the canal and the water gently reflecting the moonlight, Elspeth felt the romance of the moment. It was more than a few minutes until they parted again.

Stephen smiled broadly. "You really are something, Elspeth," he said. "Right, so I'll see you next Thursday to do the work on *The Blue Belle*. And you've got my number if you want me for anything in the meantime." He glanced along the towpath. "Looks like mum and dad are still up; I can see lights on *The Marian*. I'll pop in now – might even bunk up there for the night. See you, Elspeth."

"See you, Stephen. Thanks for a great evening."

As Elspeth let herself in to *The Blue Belle* and got ready for bed, she reflected that she still wasn't *entirely* sure what to make of Stephen's intentions towards her. The kiss had certainly been enjoyable, but he hadn't suggested a further date, and had wandered off down the towpath to see Mary and Ian: *hardly* the actions of a man passionately enamoured with a new love. Elspeth wasn't sure that she was necessarily *passionately* enamoured either. She definitely clicked with Stephen; he was great fun and certainly attractive, but she wasn't sure whether there was any more to it than that. After her break up with

128

Peter, Elspeth was determined to make sure that her next relationship, whatever and whenever it might be, would be what she really wanted, not what she thought she *should* want. She smiled at her tendency to get ahead of herself: she and Stephen had enjoyed one brief kiss; he hadn't exactly asked her to marry him. Resolving not to overthink things and to try to enjoy being a single woman who may or may not kiss electricians or go for drinks with solicitors as the mood took her, Elspeth snuggled down into her bed, grimacing briefly when she remembered that she *still* hadn't managed to change the mattress that Janice had such fond memories of, and fell asleep with the gentle motion of the boat on the water.

It was two days' after her kiss with Stephen that Elspeth's drink with Henry appeared on her calendar. She had mixed feelings about it. On the one hand, she was confident that she would have an enjoyable evening with Henry. Elspeth had no doubt that Henry was kind and intelligent, plus his company was utterly undemanding, meaning she could relax and be herself. Yet Elspeth felt a little unsure about how to approach the evening. She hadn't been single for three years, and she wasn't confident in how to manage Henry's – or her own – expectations. Should she tell Henry about Stephen? Or would that signal an assumption that she thought Henry should tell her about anyone else *he* was seeing? And was this even a romantic date in the first place? Perhaps Henry simply saw Elspeth as a friend. Elspeth decided to approach the evening casually, donning jeans, a t-shirt and trainers as she got ready, and resolved not to mention Stephen unless it either came up naturally or Henry broached the possibility of them dating exclusively.

Arriving at the welcoming but unassuming pub to see Henry already settled at a table with a pint, Elspeth immediately felt at ease. Henry looked smart, in a white shirt and jeans, but had worn his glasses for the evening, a sign to Elspeth that he felt comfortable enough with her that he didn't need to fuss about with his irritating contact lenses. He offered to buy Elspeth a drink, and she accepted on the understanding that she would buy the next round. The conversation was relaxed and open, and Elspeth was happy to listen as Henry talked about his reflections on his now-finished relationship with Amy. It appeared that some of Amy's comments had hit home, and he was, a little like Elspeth, in the process of re-evaluating who he was and what he wanted outside of a relationship. "The thing is, I can see what Amy meant about wanting me to be more assertive. But on the other hand, I don't want to change myself for somebody else, you know? I guess I just have to figure out what I want to work on for me?"

Elspeth nodded. Henry was certainly on the more emotionally open side than Peter and it was refreshing to hear his perspective. She found herself talking through some of the realisations that she'd had after her own break up. "I know exactly what you mean," she said. "When I was with Peter, I was always trying to be more sensible to please him. But after we split up, I realised that it's important for me to do it because *I* want to, not for somebody else. I guess the key is deciding which aspects are valuable to me. I mean, being sensible in terms of taking charge of my own finances definitely *is* important, but perhaps watching documentaries *isn't* really something I want to work on," she grinned.

By the end of the evening, Elspeth felt lighter and brighter for her conversation with Henry. She had warmed even more to his somewhat awkward and hesitant charm, and as they left the pub she wondered fleetingly whether she would like him to put his arm around her and kiss her in the way Stephen had done two nights before. As they lingered in the pub carpark, Elspeth reflected that this was somewhat irrelevant; Henry simply wouldn't be assertive in that way. If anything were going to happen between them romantically, Elspeth would need to be the one to initiate it. She decided that she wasn't *sure* enough about Henry to do that; not yet, anyway. But as they parted, Elspeth was left with a warm, affectionate feeling. Whatever may or may not happen between them, Elspeth was certainly glad that her inheritance of *The Blue Belle* had brought Henry Green into her life. And, she thought with a smile, she was glad it had brought Stephen Parker into her life too. Two evenings out with two good-looking, interesting, single men in one week; now *that* was a new one for Elspeth. It was exciting to think that there were possibilities.

Chapter 15: Progress

As promised, Stephen came to do the electrical work on *The Blue Belle* the following week. His demeanour was as friendly and easy-going as it had been the first time they met, and Elspeth couldn't help but mentally contrast him with Henry. Watching Stephen confidently tackle the practical tasks on *The Blue Belle*, Elspeth thought that there was something very attractive about someone who was so utterly assured in everything they said and did. Stephen might not have Henry's sensitive, introspective nature, but that had its advantages. They worked amiably alongside each other for the morning, Stephen on the electrical upgrades while Elspeth touched up any spots of rust on the boat's interior shell with Vactan, and Elspeth found herself thoroughly enjoying the feeling of working alongside somebody on what had so far been a completely solo project. They chatted as they worked, and Stephen gave Elspeth all sorts of useful information about the reality of living on a narrow boat, gleaned from the years of helping his parents on *The Marian*.

Breaking for lunch at around one o'clock, Elspeth made them a simple lunch of cheese and tomato sandwiches which they ate together, snuggled closely on the small seat on the prow of *The Blue Belle*. Elspeth felt somehow energised by Stephen's presence, but was still at a loss as to whether he saw her romantically or not. They worked more slowly for their afternoon shift, both tiring as the day went on due to the physical nature of their tasks, and at around four o'clock Stephen announced that the electrical works were complete. He refused to take any payment for the labour, charging Elspeth only for the basic materials, and promised to come over again once she had completed the next major task on her agenda – the tedious and challenging task of insulating the interior of the boat – to have a look over the engine bay with her and check everything was in good order.

Elspeth wondered whether Stephen would suggest another meal at the pub, but as he was leaving he mentioned that he was out with his mates that night for a curry. Elspeth found herself slightly relieved; it answered the question for her and meant that she didn't have the dilemma of whether to mention her recent date with Henry. As she waved Stephen off down the towpath, watching his strong frame effortlessly wielding his enormous tool box, Elspeth reflected that he certainly *was* an attractive prospect as a partner. She just wasn't sure whether she wanted to pursue anything like that with him; at least not yet.

The completion of the electrical work meant that Elspeth could start on the next stage of her renovation the following day: a job that she had been simultaneously eagerly anticipating and dreading. The insulation. After much research, Elspeth had opted to install insulation boards, primarily so that she could continue living on *The Blue Belle* while she did the work, and secondarily because it was fractionally cheaper than spray insulation. The drawback was that it would be a big job – she had estimated three weeks in her schedule of works. What with her shifts at *The Waterside*, it was going to be physically gruelling. But, she reminded herself, this was real progress. It was the first time that she would be bringing things *in* to *The Blue Belle* rather than taking them *out*. And, she reminded herself, every insulation board she fitted was an investment in her future cosiness and happiness on *The Blue Belle*. Plus, she was giving the boat a bit of love, as Reggie would have put it.

As predicted, the work was demanding and tedious. Elspeth had booked a delivery for half of the insulation boards to be delivered on the first week, as she knew that she would be unable to store them all on the boat and wanted to avoid asking Janice for the use of her spare room for storage if at all possible. As Elspeth measured, cut and fitted the boards, she fell into a rhythm and became fairly efficient, yet it was a struggle to keep motivated as the scale of the task was huge and doing it alone meant that her progress was slow. She found that she was grateful for her currently regular weekday lunchtime shifts at the café, as they gave a structure to her day. She would get up at eight, be dressed in her work clothes by nine, then work for two hours on the insulation boarding before having a quick shower and starting at the café for eleven thirty to start her three hour weekday shift. Arriving back on *The Blue Belle* around two, she would sometimes treat herself to a brief rest before resuming her work on the boarding, and getting in another three hours before finishing for the day. Hour by hour, day by day, then eventually week by week, the interior of *The Blue Belle* was transformed into a shiny, silver shell of insulation boarding. When Elspeth went to sleep at night, she dreamt of huge halls filled with stacks and stacks of boards that needed to be cut, and had nightmares about expanding foam that simply would not do as it was bid. But eventually, just slightly over her three week schedule, Elspeth sat on the hard cushion over the water-tank feeling a sense of achievement. Her insulation was finished. And, she had to admit, she was proud of the work she had done. For a complete novice, she had done her research, she had not cut corners and she had made a tidy job of it. She decided to call her friends to see if any of them fancied meeting up – she felt she had cause to celebrate.

To Elspeth's delight, Minnie, Ava and Nina were all free that Friday night and keen to meet for a drink at *The Duck Inn*. Elspeth was relieved that Nina seemed to fit in perfectly with her other close friends, and so rather than gaining one friend after her appeal to Elspeth, Nina had gained three. From the sounds of it, each of the women had their own reasons for wanting to come out for the evening: Nina was up against it at work and was apparently having some issues with her nanny, Minnie had just broken up with her most recent boyfriend, and Ava had some news she wanted to share. Cosy in their corner booth, Minnie was the first to offload after a few gulps of her wine.

"He had a fiancée *all along*!" she revealed incredulously. "Can you imagine? What on earth she thought was going on is beyond me. I mean, imagine not realising that your fiancée is seeing another woman! He was at my flat at least two nights a week. Oh, sorry, Elspeth."

"What? *Oh*, you mean Peter and Maria. Well, I suppose that didn't go on for that long. But still, I know what you mean. So how did you find out?"

Minnie rolled her eyes. "Our mothers. Would you believe it? Turns out they know each other from Thursday morning Pilates at the village hall. My mum was talking about how her daughter was seeing a roofer called Pete, then her friend April says, *oh, isn't that funny, my son's a roofer called Pete too!*

What a coincidence. Then they kept talking and realised that it wasn't the sort of coincidence they thought it was and that *actually* Pete is a lying piece of you-know-what. So, obviously my mum calls me and tells me all about it – I think it was the most dramatic thing that's *ever* happened at Pilates and all the women there got involved – and I confronted him."

"What did he say?" asked Nina, her eyes wide at the drama.

"Well, it was all a bit pathetic, really. At first he went on about how I'm the one he really loves, how he's going to break it off with her, blah blah blah, so I called him out on it and suggested we ring her there and then. Obviously he wouldn't. I pushed it a bit – not that I *really* had any intention of staying with him after that – then eventually he just gave up and said that actually, he couldn't split up with her after all. Already got a joint mortgage and had talked about plans to have children, all that stuff. Said I was a bit of a final fling before the wedding. He actually tried to pull the sympathy card – how hard it was for him to have to be faithful to one woman – like I should feel sorry for him! And goodness knows what his mum's going to do about it; no idea whether she'll tell the fiancée or not. I wouldn't want to have *that* particular moral dilemma. So," Minnie took another big gulp of her wine. "That's it for Pete the roofer. And I need a drink tonight."

After much sympathetic murmuring about Minnie's plight, it was Nina's turn to offload. "So, it's not exactly a moral dilemma ... but it *is* a dilemma. I need your advice, girls." Elspeth, Ava and Minnie nodded sagely, all ears. "It's about my nanny. So, just for a bit of context, my nanny is a *good* nanny. As in, she's pretty reliable, she knows what she's doing with the kids, she knows our routines and all that. It's very hard to find somebody like that. Trust me." The girls nodded. If anyone understood the challenges of finding a good nanny, it would be Nina. "But," Nina continued dramatically, "I've found out that she isn't altogether honest."

Elspeth raised her eyebrows. "Not *honest*? In what way?"

"Well, here's the deal. I've got some nice stuff, right? I mean, that's my indulgence. I hardly go on holidays abroad, I don't have a big house or anything like that, but my *stuff* is my treat to myself for working so hard. I've got expensive jewellery, designer bags, designer dresses. You know. And it's been *disappearing*. Temporarily, at least. I first noticed it a few months ago, when I couldn't find my Gucci handbag. I thought maybe I'd just misplaced it; I mean, in a house with three children that's easy enough to do. Then I found it about a week later, in the place I'd looked for it to start with! I didn't think much of it at the time, just, you know, maybe I hadn't looked properly. Anyway, it's happened a few times since – with dresses, jewellery, even once with a bra! Although I'm hoping that one really *was* an oversight on my part. Then, one day last week, I *saw* her!"

"What did you see?" Ava was gripped by Nina's story.

"I was walking past that swanky new wine bar; you know, the one in town?"

Elspeth nodded grimly, recalling her soggy, jilted bride moment. "I know the one. That's where I saw Peter with Maria."

"Oh! Yes, I remember now. OK, so that one. I was walking past with the children after we'd been out for pizza one evening, and I saw my nanny through the window. It looked like she was on a date with an older man. And guess what she was wearing?"

The girls waited with baited breath.

"*My* blue Dior dress, *my* Miu Miu satin heeled pumps and *my* Hermes necklace, and carrying *my* Gucci bag! About three thousand pounds worth of *my* stuff! The cheek of it!"

"And you're sure the things were yours?" prompted Ava. "There's no chance they just looked similar?"

Nina nodded vehemently. "I'm certain. I went straight home and checked my wardrobe. It was all missing. I mean, I probably wouldn't have noticed it if I hadn't gone to look specifically; it's not as if I usually wear all my designer stuff on a regular basis. It's only because I saw her that I've rumbled her little scheme. And then, when I checked again yesterday, it's all back where it was."

"I wonder why she's doing it?" pondered Minnie. "Do you think she's trying to bag a rich man or something?"

"I wondered that," agreed Nina. "It fits, judging from the man she was with at the wine bar. He certainly looked like he was worth a bit."

"Ooh, maybe she's living some sort of double life ... nanny by day, *femme fatale* by night ..." Minnie clearly had a vivid imagination.

"Or maybe she just likes the designer clothes," suggested Elspeth sensibly. "I mean, it doesn't do anything for me, but some people love that kind of stuff. And if she can't afford it herself, which I'm guessing she can't on a nanny's wage, and the stuff's sitting there in your closet, it must be tempting. I'm not saying that makes it alright, obviously, but perhaps there's nothing more to it than that."

Ava nodded. "So what are you going to do, Nina? Can't you just ask her about it? You know, tell her you saw her and ask her what's going on?"

Nina shook her head slowly. "I thought about that," she said, "but I think the minute we have that conversation, the possibility of her working as my nanny is over. I mean, she's essentially broken the trust of the relationship and she *is* stealing, albeit temporarily, from her employer."

"So you're going to fire her?" asked Elspeth. She knew, from experience, that Nina had no problem with doing this.

"I thought about that, too," she said. "But honestly, I don't think I could manage without her. It's *because* I can rely on her – with the kids I mean – that I can commit to my job and make such good money in the first place. Good nannies are worth their weight in gold. I think I'm just going to need to have a somewhat literal take on that."

"So you're just going to let her get away with it?" asked Minnie incredulously.

"I *think* so," said Nina. "For now. Anyway, I'm intrigued to find out more about what she's up to. I think me and the kids might be taking a few more evening walks over the next few weeks!"

The conversation moved on from the case of the mysterious nanny and onto Ava's news. She looked excited as she shyly revealed that her and Matt were moving in together the next week. Things were getting serious and she thought that he might propose soon. It would be the first time that Ava had lived with a partner, and she had been building up to it slowly for some time; Matt had been staying over half the week at her flat anyway, so now seemed like the right time. The girls were delighted for her, and Elspeth felt a slight twinge of sadness as she remembered her own excitement at moving in with Peter in their little rented flat. Well, that was all in the past now, and she reminded herself that she was, on the whole, happier for it.

"So Elspeth," offered Ava. "You said you had something to celebrate too! That's why we've all come out in the first place. What's your news?"

"Well," beamed Elspeth, "It's been a tiring few weeks, but ..." she paused for effect, "I've finished the insulation boarding on *The Blue Belle*!"

Elspeth waited in vain for her friends' gasps of delight and congratulations. Instead, they exchanged glances in silence.

"Is that code for something?" Minnie whispered to Ava and Nina.

"I don't think so," returned Nina flatly. "I think that really is her news."

"Oh. Oh dear." Minnie shook her head. "I'm not sure it's good for her, spending all that time alone on an old boat. She's losing perspective."

"I can *hear* you!" interrupted Elspeth. "Seriously! OK, so maybe it's not as exciting as cheating boyfriends or scheming nannies or moving in together, but *still*. It's a massive achievement for me. I don't think it's too much to ask for my friends to be supportive."

"You're right, Elspeth. It's not," soothed Ava. "Well done. It's amazing that you've taken this project on and you're making so much progress. I genuinely couldn't do it. So, has anything else been going on for you?"

Elspeth realised that actually, there *had* been plenty going on in her life that the girls would be interested in; it was just that the fit out of *The Blue Belle* was at the forefront of her mind. "Well, yes," she said. "Actually, I've met someone. Maybe. Well, two people. Maybe. I don't know."

Now her friends were interested. She found herself telling them all about Henry; how they had gone on one unofficial and one official date, how he seemed kind and intelligent but a little lacking in confidence and assertiveness, about his high rise intonation habit ... Then she found herself telling them all about Stephen; about how they had clicked immediately when he came to do the work on *The Blue Belle*, about their meal at the pub, about the kiss on the towpath when he walked her back to her boat. As she talked, she realised what utterly different prospects Henry and Stephen were romantically, and reflected that she genuinely didn't know which one she found more appealing. When she talked about Henry, she found herself warming to the idea of him as a potential boyfriend with a feeling akin to tenderness, yet when she talked about Stephen, she found herself thinking how much fun it would be to date him and the prospect felt exciting. Hmm ... still, it was nice to think that there might be options.

"So, you're playing the field, then, Elspeth?" said Nina.

Elspeth paused. Was she? She didn't really like the term and she certainly didn't want to mess anybody about, but she *was* single and exploring her options. "I suppose I am," she agreed.

Nina grinned. "Good for you," she said. "And if you happen to find any spare men on your way, do send one in my direction."

"Mine too," Minnie piped up from behind her wineglass.

Chapter 16: Grumpy Café Man

Elspeth was feeling buoyant as she arrived for work at the café that morning. Her restoration of *The Blue Belle* was progressing beautifully and, after the dust, destruction and generally mucky work of the rip out and the upgrades to the amenities, the process of fitting out the narrow boat was incredibly satisfying. With the insulation installed and the plaster boarding now well underway, she was starting to see how her new home would come together, and every day she made visible, tangible progress. The café was busy; it was relatively warm for October, and many of the customers chose to sit outside at the picnic tables on grass next to the towpath. Elspeth was humming to herself as she cleared some of the outdoor tables, when she heard a friendly barking behind her. She would recognise that bark anywhere.

Depositing her clearing tray on the nearest table, Elspeth whirled around to greet her little canine friend. The small, cute looking dog came bounding towards her, its big, soulful eyes delighted to see Elspeth. Elspeth dropped to her knees to fuss the dog, who placed its muddy paws straight onto Elspeth's lap and gazed adoringly into her face. Elspeth fell into the sing-song, childish voice she always used with animals she felt a connection to, and began their chat. "It's so good to see you! I didn't know where you lived so I wasn't sure I'd meet you again after you came onto my boat," Elspeth cooed while she ruffled the dog's ears. "And I thought maybe you were with that *gwumpy* man. Wasn't he a *gwumpy* man? Yes, he was! He was a ..."

Elspeth trailed off as she noticed the heavy, muddy work boots in her peripheral vision. Of course. The dog *had been* with the grumpy man. The dog was *still with* the grumpy man – it obviously hadn't decided to pop to the café for an apple turnover and a latte on its own. Elspeth looked up furtively from her kneeling position, noting the yellow, high vis trousers and jacket first, then moving her gaze upwards to look at the man's face. There was no dripping yellow rain hat this time, so she could see him clearly. Elspeth had to stop herself from gasping in surprise. She had imagined him to be middle aged, perhaps with some sort of ill-advised moustache. How wrong she had been. The man looking down quizzically at Elspeth was around her age, and was, she had to admit, very handsome. His green eyes were intense and his facial hair was more designer stubble than embarrassing moustache. His hair, released from the confines of its awful yellow rainhat, was thick and dark. Elspeth felt her heart rate increase as she stared at him. Oh dear.

"Don't let me interrupt you," he said, his voice a little hard-edged. "I believe you were just bad-mouthing me to my dog. Please continue."

"What? No! Oh, you mean what I was saying about the grumpy man? No, that's *another* man. A man over there," Elspeth gestured weakly to an elderly gentleman happily tucking into a cup of tea and a bacon sandwich.

"Right. I see. Yes, he looks like a terror," returned the man drily. "So, I see you've met Daphne?"

Elspeth nearly laughed out loud. "Your dog's called *Daphne*?"

"Yes. What's wrong with that? It's a perfectly good name for a dog."

"Well, I mean ... *Daphne* ... Oh, is she named after the character in Scooby Doo?"

"No," the man said slowly, looking at Elspeth as if she had just landed from Mars. "She's actually named after Daphne from Greek mythology. She was a naiad who was turned into a laurel to protect her from the advances of Apollo. I found Daphne," he nodded to the small dog, which had now wandered away from Elspeth and was sniffing some plants with interest, "abandoned under a laurel bush when she was a puppy. The name seemed appropriate. But I guess you disagree."

"Oh right! Daphne the *naiad*." Elspeth felt suddenly very ignorant. What on earth was a *naiad*? "Obviously. I mean, that would have been my second guess."

"Obviously. Right, well, I guess me and *Daphne* had better be going. Are you ... are you alright down there?"

Elspeth realised that she was still kneeling on the slightly damp, muddy grass where she had greeted Daphne. She had been so surprised by the man's appearance that she hadn't got up, and now she realised that her right leg had gone to sleep a little. She wasn't confident that she *could* stand up now if she tried. "Yes, I'm fine. Very comfortable."

"OK. It's just – well, most people would probably have got up by now. But I guess you're not most people. Well. I'll leave you to ... whatever it is that you're doing." The man gave Elspeth a last appraising glance before setting off along the towpath with Daphne pottering behind him, the little dog occasionally pausing for a good sniff of something or other.

Elspeth crawled to a nearby picnic table and hauled herself up to sit on the bench while the

144

circulation slowly returned to her leg. *What an idiot*, she thought. Then she realised that she wasn't entirely sure *who* she was calling the idiot. Clearly, that man was very rude. He had shouted at her to move her boat on that first morning – although, as Elspeth now realised, his advice *was* compliant with Section 14.5 (a) of the terms and conditions of a Waterside Mooring contract - and now he had patronised her. Just because she didn't know all of the weird mythology references that *he* did, it didn't mean she wasn't intelligent! How dare he! But then, as Elspeth's composure returned and, with it, her sense of fairness, she had to admit that the man had been right about her not having the right to stay on the mooring that day. Plus, it *had* been utterly foul weather; enough to put anybody in a bad mood. And just now he had overheard her criticising him to his own dog. And she *had* implied that Daphne was a ridiculous name. Elspeth grimaced. While it didn't excuse his rudeness, she had to admit that she hadn't exactly conducted *herself* with decorum in their interactions. And why did he have to be so *ridiculously* attractive?

Her right leg now fully recovered, Elspeth picked up her clearing tray and made her way glumly back into the café. Her buoyant mood of this morning had evaporated: she felt silly and immature. Making her way to the kitchen at the back of the café to drop off the dirty plates, she saw Anna, who was buttering bread at lightning speed.

"You spoke to him!" exclaimed Anna.

"What?"

"The gorgeous guy from the CRT. He's never spoken to any of us. We've seen him in here a few times. He's so mysterious. He looks like he should be in a film or something, not messing about on canals in overalls all day. What did you talk about?"

"Oh, um, naiads," said Elspeth.

"Neigh ads?" repeated Anna. "Never heard of them. Are they something to do with horses?"

"Yes, maybe," muttered Elspeth distractedly. So the man came into the café regularly. Oh dear. She *really* didn't want to have another interaction with him. The more she thought about her behaviour just now, and on *The Blue Belle* the previous month, the more mortified she felt. Elspeth reflected that for some reason she'd felt far better about her initial meeting with him when his face had been obscured by his terrible hat and she had been able to imagine him as some sort of officious old busybody. The fact that, as Anna had helpfully pointed out, he looked more like he'd just stepped off a film set was really very inconvenient. Elspeth sighed as she glanced down at her work apron and the mud-stained knees of her jeans. What a sight she must look. And that first morning, yelling at him through the window to leave her alone, then appearing on the prow in the pouring rain with her soaking wet dressing gown clinging to her ... he must think she was absolutely bizarre. Resolving to think positively, Elspeth brightened at the thought that the mooring fee was all sorted now, presumably thanks to Reggie, and that thanks to Mary she now knew how to move the boat in an emergency. The grumpy but annoyingly gorgeous man *shouldn't* have any more reason to call on her. She could simply put him out of her mind, and if she ever spotted him at *The Waterside*, she planned to take the coward's way out and hide.

Chapter 17: Achievement

Elspeth was delighted at her progress on *The Blue Belle*. With the electrics upgraded, plastering completed, floor sanded and kitchen units painted, the interior of the boat was really beginning to come together. There would be longer term projects, of course: Elspeth hadn't attempted to re-fit the boat's outdated but functional bathroom, and she knew that at some point she would need to tackle the enormous job of re-painting the outside of the boat, but her project for the last few months had been to make the inside of *The Blue Belle* a cosy, inviting and functional space for her to live in. She could see that she was well on her way to doing this, and now it was time for the most exciting part, in Elspeth's view: finishing and furnishing her living space.

Elspeth was a dab hand with textiles, having been trained in various techniques as part of her art course, and she planned to save money by sourcing end of roll fabrics and doing all of the labour herself. There were three main tasks: Venetian blinds for each of the canal boat's small rectangular windows, curtaining to separate the saloon from the berth of *The Blue Belle*, and a project to create large, squishy cushions that could be positioned on top of the water tank in the saloon to create a comfortable sofa. Elspeth's trusty sewing machine was one of the few items she had kept in her big clear out, and she now liberated it from its box where it had been safely stored while the main building work was going on, and set it up on a little folding table in the saloon. Now she just needed some materials.

Making her way to the fabric market in the town centre, where she knew she would find the best prices, Elspeth spent a delightful morning browsing possible options. She eventually chose a smooth, cotton fabric in a plain white for the sofa-cushions; she knew that white wasn't the most practical choice, but the image of the boat's interior in her mind's eye *absolutely* had white sofa cushions nestled against the sage green backdrop of the walls, so there was no question about her choice. Elspeth reasoned that she could insert zips in the cushion covers and, as they were cotton, they would be machine washable if there were any spillages. She then found a delightful light fabric with a delicate pattern of green leaves and daisies, perfect for the window blinds. A heavy floral damask in complementary tones would serve as a curtain to insulate the berth in the winter months, while a swathe of white batiste would be used to create a semi-transparent curtain for the cooler summer months and as a partial screen. Elspeth managed to buy the roll ends at very reasonable prices, which turned out to be for the best: as she rummaged in her bag, she couldn't find her bank card anywhere. Luckily, she had enough cash on her to cover her purchases, and she reminded herself to check in the pockets of her jeans when she got home for the bank card: she knew that she had a habit of shoving the card in her back pocket, so wasn't too concerned at its absence. Excited by her purchases, Elspeth made her way back to *The Blue Belle*, clutching her fabric rolls under her arm.

As she approached her mooring, Elspeth was surprised to see a man hovering next to her boat, stooping as if to peer into the windows and see if anyone was at home. She watched as he stepped onto the prow of *The Blue Belle* and knocked at the door. For a moment, Elspeth wondered whether it might be Stephen; this man had the same tall, broad shouldered build. But no, she realised as she got closer; Stephen's hair was fair, a kind of sandy brown, whereas this man was definitely dark-haired. Just as she was reaching the barge, he turned and Elspeth dropped her rolls of fabric in surprise. *Grumpy Barge Man*.

"Oh, no!" Elspeth cried in dismay as her fabric reels began rolling off in different directions. Worried they were going to make their way into the canal, she forgot her awkwardness at seeing the man again and began inelegantly chasing the fabric rolls, half crouching as she did so. Once they were all safely retrieved and tucked back under her arm, she took a breath to compose herself and went to greet her guest, who seemed to have been watching her little fabric-chasing performance with bemusement.

To her dismay, Grumpy Barge Man was not wearing his dirty overalls *or* his enormous rain hat, and consequently looked even more attractive than he had done at *The Waterside* yesterday. "Good morning," Elspeth offered in what she hoped was the tone of a normal person. "And what brings you here?"

The man looked a little disconcerted at her odd turn of phrase, but offered her a smile of sorts. If she didn't know better, Elspeth might have even thought that he seemed a little nervous.

"I found your bank card yesterday," he said awkwardly. "I went back past the café on my way home that evening and it was lying on the grass; you must've dropped it when you were fussing Daphne. The café was closed so I thought maybe I should just bring it round." He held out Elspeth's bank card as if to prove his story. "And I thought perhaps I should introduce myself properly," he continued. "I mean, we've met twice now and both times it was a bit ... you know. My boat's moored a bit further up the canal, so I guess our paths will cross now and again. I'm Alex, by the way."

Elspeth was flummoxed. This was the last thing she had expected. He had been rude to her – twice – although admittedly she had been rude to him – twice – and now here he was, doing her the favour of returning her bank card in person and seemingly wanting to be ... what was it exactly? *Neighbourly*, perhaps? *Friendly*, even? Despite her almost overwhelming urge to run away and hide behind a bush, she decided that she certainly didn't want to be rude to him again.

"I'm Elspeth," she offered awkwardly. "It's, um, nice to meet you properly, Alex. Would you like to join me for a cup of tea? I think I've got some shortbread biscuits somewhere. It's still a bit of a mess on board, but – "

"I'd like that," Alex interrupted. "I mean, if that's alright?"

"Of course. Let me just find my key." Elspeth fumbled in her bag while trying to balance the fabric rolls, until Alex gallantly took them from her, brushing his arm against hers in the process. Elspeth found herself acutely aware of the brief physical contact and was glad when they were on board *The Blue Belle* and she had placed the fabric rolls safely on the kitchen worktop so there would be no need for any further close proximity. As Elspeth put the kettle on and rummaged in the newly-painted cupboards for the shortbread biscuits, Alex gazed in surprise around the interior of the small boat.

"It's all looking very new and fresh in here," he commented. "What have you had done?"

"A lot," said Elspeth with a smile, as they took a seat on the old, hard sofa with their tea. "I ripped out the old cladding – it looked a bit like a sauna in here – then I found that the insulation could do with replacing, so I took that out and addressed any rust patches with Vactan. I had someone in to look at the electrics, which are thankfully in pretty good shape, then I boarded and plastered. Obviously I've sanded and painted the kitchen units too. So now it's the fun bit!" Elspeth smiled and took a sip of her warm tea. "I'm painting the walls over the next couple of days, then doing the soft furnishings this week and next – you know, blinds, curtains and some new sofa cushions. That's why my trusty sewing machine has come out of retirement." She nodded to where it sat waiting on its little foldaway table.

Alex looked at Elspeth in amazement. "You keep saying *I*," he said. "You don't mean to tell me that you've done all of this *by yourself*?"

Elspeth nodded. "Yep. Apart from the electrical upgrades. I needed someone qualified for that. But the rest of it I've done myself."

"Wow." Alex seemed genuinely impressed. "That's a huge project to take on, Elspeth. And the insulation boards? I need to upgrade the insulation at some point on my boat, but I just can't bring myself to start a project on that scale. It must've taken you weeks."

"Just over three weeks," Elspeth nodded, a warm feeling washing over her that *someone* understood the scale of her project. She remembered her friends' utterly unimpressed expressions when she had told them about her progress with the work. It was gratifying to talk to Alex about it.

"So, you have your own boat?" she prompted.

Alex nodded. "Yes. *The Briar Rose*. I used to live on it with my dad, until he passed away a few years ago. Anyway, now it's just me. I mean, I like it, I suppose. It's the only life I've ever really known. I know a fair bit about canal boats, as you can imagine. And now I work for the CRT. Anyway," he stood up and brushed the shortbread crumbs from his (Elspeth couldn't help but notice) nicely fitted jeans. "I should be going. I can see you've got plenty of things to be getting on with. I just ... well, I just wanted to make sure you got your bank card back. And if you need any help or advice about *The Blue Belle*, you could always ask me. I could give you my number, if you like?" he offered shyly.

"Yes! Definitely. Where's my phone ..." muttered Elspeth, rummaging desperately in her bag but unable to find it. "Never mind. Could you jot it down for me?" She handed him the little pad and pencil which already had Stephen's number scrawled on it by Mary.

Alex wrote it down and handed the pad back to her. "Well, thanks for the tea. And the shortbread. I'll probably see you around," he said, making his way out of *The Blue Belle,* ducking slightly as he made his way through the door.

"Yes, see you!" returned Elspeth, trying her hardest to sound easy going and casual when she felt anything but. Alex had given her his number! It was only after she had surreptitiously watched him make his way along the towpath that she realised it might have been a decent idea to offer him hers as well. Never mind. She would find an excuse to message him soon enough. With that in mind, Elspeth began a hunt for her phone so that she could add Alex's details. It was nowhere to be found inside *The Blue Belle*, and she turned her bag inside out to see if it had made its way into a sneaky pocket. Wondering where on earth she had left it, Elspeth wandered out to the prow of the boat to clear her head, then was dismayed to feel her foot nudge against something *right* at the edge of the boat. The phone must have fallen out of Elspeth's bag as she had fumbled for the key with Alex. The succeeding *plop* as the phone met the water was no surprise, and Elspeth peered over the side at the place where her phone had disappeared into the canal. Oops.

Elspeth stood for a few minutes looking at the water, as if somehow the phone might bob back up to the surface, magically still working. It wasn't that it was an expensive phone or anything like that – rather hilariously, it was an old one of Janice's. Elspeth was aware that most people gave their parents their old phones rather than the other way around, but Janice liked to have the newest gadgets. It was one of the many ways in which she showed herself that she was 'worth it'. But Elspeth knew that it would cost a bit to replace it and, more importantly, it had all of her contacts on it. She briefly considered messaging one of her friends to ask them what they thought she should do, before realising that she obviously *couldn't* message anyone without a phone. Living alone on *The Blue Belle* as she was, Elspeth reasoned that a working phone was something of a priority for her. She resolved to postpone her original plan of starting the internal painting that afternoon and decided to make her way back into town instead. There was a shop that sold refurbished phones; Elspeth would buy the cheapest functional model that she could find and perhaps still have time to make a start on the painting later that afternoon.

A couple of hours later, putting the first strokes of fresh, sage green paint onto the wall as her newly acquired phone charged in the corner, Elspeth felt calm and purposeful. She aimed to do the first coat of one of the long walls on the boat before she stopped work for the day, and she could immediately see the difference the beautiful shade of green would make to the interior. The phone situation was annoying, but the reconditioned one had not been too expensive and Elspeth figured that she could re-populate it with her contacts soon enough. She would see Minnie, Ava and Nina the following evening for a drink at *The Duck Inn*, and planned to pop in on Janice later that week to return some of Rick's power tools, so she could ask them for their numbers then. She remembered she had Henry's work mobile on some paperwork, so could contact him via that, and of course Stephen and Alex's numbers were both written on the pad of paper in the boat. Elspeth reasoned that she could just build up her list of contact numbers slowly from there as and when she saw people.

The sage green paint made a world of difference to the interior of *The Blue Belle*, and for the next week or so Elspeth was in her element. Having finished the interior painting, she turned her attention towards her soft furnishings, and as she made and fitted each little window blind, the space became more and more cosy. There was another trip to the recycling centre for her to dispose of the old, hard sofa cushions to make space for the squishy, oversized ones that she would sew herself, and once these were in situ the space really began to take shape. After weeks of living on a building site, Elspeth could finally relax in the evenings on her sofa, thinking about the finishing touches for *The Blue Belle* and beginning to make plans for what she might do with herself once the re-fit was complete.

It was on one such evening, as Elspeth read on the sofa with a hot chocolate, that she realised she hadn't heard from Henry, Stephen or indeed *any* of her friends for a few days. Of course; they didn't have her new number. She had added theirs to her phone, but had forgotten to share her contact details. Picking up her phone from the floor next to her, she tried to send them her number. It was a fiddly phone and not particularly user-friendly; Elspeth guessed that was perhaps why it had been such a good price; perhaps everyone else knew that this particular brand wasn't exactly easy to use. Still, it did the job. She eventually managed to set up a message all and shared her new number. She was interested to see whether Henry, Stephen or even Alex might respond to say hi.

Looking around at her now almost-finished space, Elspeth thought how lovely it would be to entertain on *The Blue Belle*. As she sipped her hot chocolate, an idea began to form in her mind; she could have a barge warming! She could invite Minnie, Ava and Nina over to toast *The Blue Belle* with her. There was just about enough room on the sofa for her three guests, and she could always perch on the little foldaway table as a seat. It would be cosy. If they were free to come this Saturday, that would give Elspeth the motivation to get everything completely finished by then. She picked up her phone and typed out a message: "You are warmly invited to a barge-warming for *The Blue Belle* on Saturday 12th. Please bring a bottle and plenty of crisps! Elspeth xxxx". There. Sent. Elspeth settled back into the comfy cushions that she had made herself. She would drive into town tomorrow and go to a couple of interiors shops – she didn't need anything fancy, maybe a couple of rugs and a table lamp to make the place even more homely. Elspeth let a feeling of contentment overwhelm her as she relaxed with her book. She had achieved something that she was proud of. Thinking back to the letter she had found from Reggie, she found herself hoping that he would have liked what she had done, too. It had been a long and arduous journey, but *The Blue Belle* really did feel like home.

Chapter 18: Barge-warming

The Blue Belle looked beautiful. Elspeth had to admit that she had done a stunning job with the interior. Gone were the dark, dingy carpets, replaced with a stylish wooden floor, stained white and adorned with two pretty rugs: one placed strategically between the wood burner and the sofa to mark out the lounge area, or *saloon* as she now knew it was called, and a small runner between the two short lengths of units in the galley kitchen to create a cosy cooking space. The walls, now devoid of the sauna-esque wood cladding that had previously adorned them, were freshly plaster-boarded and painted in the calming sage-green that Elspeth had always loved so much. The wooden kitchen doors, lovingly sanded, painted in white and finished with pale green handles by Elspeth, looked delightful, while the sagging red velvet curtain that had previously separated the bedroom area had been replaced by two layers of fresh screening: a diaphanous tier of white batiste for semi-privacy and the summer months, with an additional heavier lined curtain in delicately patterned damask for privacy and added insulation in the winter. The only furniture in the main living area, aside from the fitted kitchen units and the wood-burner, was the white sofa that Elspeth had constructed with large, squishy cushions over the narrow boat's water tank and the little foldaway table, plus a small side table with a cosy lamp and selection of books and magazines. The interior of *The Blue Belle* looked double the size of the poky space that Elspeth had first encountered, and Elspeth felt delighted with what she had achieved.

Elspeth had bought some indoor and outdoor string lights to deck out the narrow boat for tonight's tiny barge warming. She hung two strands around the outside entrance to *The Blue Belle*, and used another two to adorn the windows inside. The effect of the cosy glow created by the single table lamp and the string lights was utterly magical. Elspeth went to her bedroom at the back of the boat to change, selecting the one party dress she had kept in her massive clear out and marvelling at how refreshing it was to have such a streamlined closet. All of those years with racks of clothes and she had always felt that she had nothing to wear. Now, she had just one slightly dressy evening outfit: a midnight blue, floaty dress that fell to just below her knees. If she was dressing up for the evening, that was what she would wear. The simplicity was liberating. Elspeth donned the silver sandals she had kept – even though she wouldn't be going out as such, tonight was a celebration and she wanted to complete her outfit – then added some delicate silver jewellery. There. She checked the clock on her bedside table: 7.45pm. She had another fifteen minutes before Ava, Minnie and Nina were due to arrive.

Confident that *The Blue Belle* was ready for its first guests, Elspeth put on a playlist of chilled out music to set the atmosphere. Settling down on her comfy sofa to read a book until her friends arrived, she was startled by a loud knock on the outside door of the narrow boat. Elspeth was surprised; it wasn't like them to actually be *early* to anything. Pulling herself up from the sofa, Elspeth opened the door with a wide smile to greet her friends.

"Mum! What are you doing here?"

Janice stood on the little outdoor platform of *The Blue Belle*, holding two bottles of Chardonnay and a grab bag of Monster Munch, accompanied by a rather excited looking Rick.

"Happy barge-warming!" said Rick. "We weren't sure whether to bring one bottle or two, but we thought, you know, better to be prepared!"

"Oh! Right. Thanks Rick. Erm, you'd better come in."

Elspeth stood to one side to let Rick, then Janice pass.

"This is a bit posh, isn't it, Elspeth?" said Rick, appraising the stylish interior. "She's done a lovely job of it, hasn't she, Janice?"

Elspeth glanced at her mother, wondering how she would manage to insult her on this occasion. She was surprised when Janice, looking around her with wide-eyes, said sincerely. "Yes. She really has. It's beautiful."

"Thanks mum," said Elspeth, feeling a little emotional and unsettled at receiving a compliment from Janice. "Now, Rick, why don't you take a seat while me and mum get us some drinks?"

"Right you are, Elspeth." Rick settled himself down on the sofa and picked up a copy of *Waterways World* from the side table, while Elspeth steered Janice back to the kitchen.

"Mum, what on *earth* are you doing here?" hissed Elspeth as she opened the wine.

"That's not a very nice way to greet your guests, Elspeth," Janice retorted indignantly. "*You* invited us."

"No, I didn't."

"Yes, you did. Look, I've got the text here." Janice fished her phone out of her bag and showed Elspeth a message: "You are warmly invited to a barge-warming for *The Blue Belle* on Saturday 12th.

Please bring a bottle and plenty of crisps! Elspeth xxxx"

"Oh! Oh no. Sorry mum. That was meant for Minnie, Ava and Nina. We were going to have a bit of a girls' night. I wonder why it got sent to you? I must have pressed the wrong button - I'm not used to this new phone."

Elspeth picked up her phone from the kitchen counter and checked her sent messages.

"Oh no! Oh, no no no no no!"

"What's the matter?"

"I've somehow sent this to *all* of my contacts. I must've clicked on the message I sent to everyone giving them my new phone number. That means it's gone to ..." Elspeth checked the names on the list. "You, Ava, Minnie, Nina, Henry, Stephen and ..." she gulped, "Alex."

"Well, I don't know who most of these people are, Elspeth," said Janice. "I've got my own social life to manage, you know. But I can't see why it's a problem if some of them turn up with a bottle of something and a bag of crisps."

Elspeth felt desperate. She absolutely *could* see why it was a problem. Henry and Stephen were both ... well ... *possibilities* romantically. There was nothing official with either of them yet – one drink with Henry and one kiss with Stephen didn't mean that she was about to run off into the sunset with one of them - but the idea of them being in the same room was *awkward* to say the least. And then ... *Alex*. Elspeth felt a bit sick. Obviously there was nothing romantic between *them*; but despite his neighbourly action of returning her bank card the other day, she still felt uncomfortable about her previous rudeness and reasoned that he probably still thought she was an idiot. Yet she couldn't help feeling a bit giddy when she thought of him and, she had to admit, she had hoped that maybe *somehow*, at some point, she might be able to get to know him a little better and to perhaps improve his impression of her. Clearly, this scenario would *not* help.

"Anyway," Janice continued, interrupting her thoughts. "They probably won't come. Me and Rick only came because we thought we should; you being my daughter and everything."

Elspeth exhaled. Janice was probably right. Alex was an attractive young man who hardly knew her and wasn't exactly keen on what he *did* know about her. He would probably have much better things to do with his Saturday evening than come to her barge-warming. As for Henry and Stephen ... well, Elspeth wasn't confident that either of them would turn up. It would probably just be her, Janice, Rick and the girls. It wasn't exactly the evening she'd had in mind, but still.

"OK. Well, seeing as you're here, mum, let's treat it as a party and enjoy it. And, you know, thank you. For coming. And for saying that I've done a good job with *The Blue Belle*. It means a lot."

Elspeth readied herself for a hug, only to receive a dismissive grunt from Janice who made her way to the sofa with two very generous glasses of Chardonnay for her and Rick.

A loud knock on the door told Elspeth that more of her guests had arrived. She checked the clock. Five past eight – now *that* was more in line with her expectations of her friends. Elspeth opened to door to see Ava, Minnie and Nina huddled together in the small space. "Happy barge-warming!" shouted Ava, holding up a bottle of Prosecco and a twelve pack of salt and vinegar crisps. "Love the lights!" she nodded to the pretty, colourful string lights on the deck.

"Thanks everyone," said Elspeth, leading them inside and gesturing for them to place their bottles and crisps on the wooden kitchen work surface.

"Hi Janice!" called Minnie. "I didn't know Elspeth had invited you!"

"Neither did she," returned Janice. "Nice to see you, girls. Cheers!"

"This is *gorgeous*, Elspeth," exclaimed Minnie, looking appreciatively around the small space. "I must admit, I didn't think ... well, I wasn't sure you'd be able to make it work. But this is a triumph."

"Thanks Minnie." Elspeth set about opening the prosecco. She only had two wine glasses left, having given the other two to Janice and Rick. "Sorry, Nina, we'll have to use mugs," she said with a grin.

"As long as it's got prosecco in it, that's fine with me," smiled Nina. "Gosh, it's good to be out of the house. The kids have been driving me *nuts*."

The girls continued their conversation, huddled together in the galley kitchen, with Ava particularly interested to learn from Nina about what might be involved in having a family now that she and Matt were getting more serious. Elspeth busied herself trying to fit as many of the bottles as she could into her tiny fridge, when there was another knock at the door.

Minnie looked round in surprise. "Who's that, Elspeth? I didn't know you'd invited anyone else."

"Neither did I," muttered Elspeth, going to answer the door, her heart pounding. Which one would it be?

"Henry!" Elspeth found that she was relieved. Of the three possibilities, Henry was probably the easiest to deal with. He looked rather attractive as he stood in the small doorway, silhouetted against the evening sky. He was clearly trying out his contact lenses again, and was wearing the pale blue shirt that brought out the colour of his eyes.

"Hi Elspeth," he said, a little shyly. "I wasn't sure what to bring? So I went for a bottle of Spanish Albarino? I hope that's alright?" His high rise intonation was in full flow.

"Albarino?" called Nina from the kitchen. "I *love* Albarino! Can I try a glass, well, a mug, with you after I finish this prosecco?"

"Oh! Of course. That would be lovely. I'm glad I've brought something people will like?"

"Thanks Henry. That's perfect. Come on in and I'll introduce you to everyone."

Henry squeezed into the galley kitchen with the girls, and was immediately pounced on with questions from all three. What did he do? How did he know Elspeth? Was he *very* knowledgeable about wine? Elspeth smiled to herself as she poured Henry a mug of Alberino and emptied the crisps her guests had bought into bowls. Henry seemed delighted by the interest from her friends – and why not? Another knock at the door claimed her attention. Just two possibilities left. Which would it be?

"Stephen!" Elspeth found her reaction was mixed this time. On the one hand, she felt far more comfortable around Stephen than she would around Alex, but there was the slightly difficult fact that she was *sort of* involved with Stephen and *sort of* involved with Henry. Hmm. She would just have to hope that the two of them didn't interact with each other too much – well, she doubted that they'd be able to get a word in edgeways with Minnie, Ava and Nina there anyway. On the other hand, she realised that she had *almost* been hoping it was Alex. She didn't know what on earth she would say to him if she saw him and the whole thing would be horrendously awkward, but ... she realised that she wanted to see him nonetheless. Turning her attention to Stephen, Elspeth gave him a bright smile.

"Hey Elspeth! Looks like a cool party," said Stephen, peering past her into the small interior of the boat. "I've never been to a barge-warming before. How many people do you think you can fit on here?"

"Erm, I think we're probably about up to capacity now!" said Elspeth, wondering how on earth Stephen, who at six foot two would only just fit under the ceiling's head height, was going to squeeze onto the barge at all, what with Janice and Rick comfortably ensconced on the sofa and barely any standing room left in the galley kitchen. She needn't have worried. As Elspeth stood back to welcome Stephen in, he immediately made himself at home in the kitchen, depositing the clearly cheap bottle emblazoned with "White Wine" he had brought on the worktop, before confidently striking up conversation with Elspeth's friends and Henry as if he had known them for years. He helped himself to a mug of wine from the open bottle of Chardonnay that Janice and Rick had brought, before joining Rick and Janice in the small sitting room and sitting cross legged on the rug. Positioning himself between the two groups somehow changed the dynamic; rather than two separate spaces, the interior of the boat somehow became one social area, and the conversation began to flow across *The Blue Belle* between all of Elspeth's guests. As she moved around her small space, she heard Minnie and Rick chatting about Minnie's new job, Stephen and Janice talking about the healing power of crystals, and Nina and Henry comparing their legal careers. Elspeth would never have expected it, but the eclectic combination of individuals and the cosy, limited space on the barge were somehow conducive to social interaction. She was just beginning to relax into the atmosphere when a loud knock on the door made her jump. Surely not. She glanced at the clock. It was eight forty-five. Not *ridiculously* late to turn up to a party that had started at eight.

Excusing herself from her conversation with Ava, who went to join Janice and Stephen, Elspeth opened the door, her heart beating inconveniently loudly. Sure enough, there he was, an imposing figure in the doorway.

"Alex! Hi! I, erm, I didn't think you would come."

"No. Well. I wasn't sure whether I should. I was quite surprised that you invited me, to be honest. I mean, I know we haven't exactly ..." Alex trailed off.

"No. I know. Well, I'm ... I'm glad you're here," said Elspeth simply. Despite the awkwardness and the embarrassment she felt at seeing him, it was the truth. They stood self-consciously for a moment before Elspeth remembered that it was customary to invite your guests in. There was an inept dance as she tried to stand to the side of the door frame to usher him in at the same time as Alex put his hand out to indicate Elspeth should go first, resulting in her stepping backwards into his open arms.

"Oh. Sorry. I didn't mean to –"

"No. Me neither. Sorry. You go first."

And with that, Alex was on *The Blue Belle* as well. Squeezing into the galley kitchen with him to help him to a drink, Elspeth brushed up against him and found herself to be uncomfortably hot despite her floaty dress. She took a gulp of her prosecco to calm her nerves.

"So, we've got Prosecco, Chardonnay, some indiscriminate 'White Wine', Alberino and – thank you," she took the bottle that Alex proffered, "now a Chablis as well. What would you like?"

"I'll have whatever's open," said Alex. "I'm not fussy about that kind of thing."

"OK then, let's go for the Chardonnay. I'll just get you a glass ..." Elspeth began, before realising that she had run out of glasses ages ago. "Sorry, no glasses left. I mean a mug ..." Peering into the cupboard, Elspeth realised that they were out of mugs too. "Oh. Right." Rummaging in the cupboard, Elspeth realised that she only had some delicate floral tea-cups left as drinking vessels. Well, she hadn't exactly planned on entertaining *eight people* this evening. She picked out a tea cup, filled it with wine and gave it to a slightly perplexed Alex.

"That's an ... interesting way to serve it," he said, trying to hold the tiny handle of the tea cup in his large hands. He took a delicate sip. "Thanks. That's ... weird."

"You're welcome," said Elspeth, feeling a little panicked. A part of her had wanted Alex to come, but now that he was here she had no idea what she was actually going to *do* with him all evening. She surveyed her guests, wondering who was the least problematic one to introduce him to. As it turned out, she needn't have bothered. A loud voice cut across the small boat.

"Alex! What are you doing here?"

"Janice! It's been ages. How are things?" To Elspeth's astonishment, Alex slipped past her and went to greet her mother on the sofa, squeezing in next to Janice as if they were old friends.

Chapter 19: Combinations

The unassuming *Blue Belle* was now absolutely full to capacity, and Elspeth had lost any hope of managing the social interactions of her guests. The alcohol was in full flow, the Monster Munch and salt and vinegar crisps were being demolished at an alarming rate, and the most surprising social combinations were revealing themselves. Elspeth's guests clearly all felt very comfortable on the narrow boat; almost a little *too* comfortable. They were moving around into all of the available spaces in a way that Elspeth found quite frankly alarming. Elspeth had already walked into the tiny shower room to find Nina and Henry deep in conversation, Nina perched on the toilet seat with the lid down and Henry sitting cross-legged in the base of the shower. She had then gone to her bedroom to re-apply her lipstick to find Rick and Stephen chilling out on the bed like teenagers, flicking through the back issues of *Canal Boat Magazine* that Elspeth had found on the boat and comparing notes on the best brand for drill bits. It was all a bit much.

Strangest, though, was the situation on the sofa with Alex and Janice. Elspeth hadn't ventured over to them yet – the idea of simultaneously facing Janice's critical comments and Alex's potentially patronising tone was unappealing to say the least. Yet Elspeth was itching to know what on earth they were talking about. Keeping an eye on them surreptitiously as she chatted to Minnie and Ava in a little cluster in the galley kitchen, she spied an opportunity when Alex went to use the bathroom. *Good luck getting Henry and Nina out of there*, she thought to herself.

Elspeth excused herself from the group in the kitchen and slipped onto the sofa next to Janice.

"How do you know Alex?" she hissed. Time was of the essence. She needed to be direct.

"Through Reggie, of course. Alex's dad, Paul, and Reggie were best friends." Janice's eyes misted up briefly. "Oh, he was a laugh, was Paul. We had some great times. He had a bit of a thing for me as well, you know. But I was all for Reggie."

"And maybe a bit for my dad as well? I mean, you were still technically married ..."

"Well, *technically*. Anyway, Reggie and Paul were always close. Like brothers, really. So when I came up to see Reggie we'd sometimes spend a bit of time with Paul and Alex as well, what with them mooring a few boats up from *The Blue Belle*. I suppose I'm like a mother to Alex," said Janice dramatically.

"I thought you said you and Reggie used to meet on Mondays," said Elspeth. "Surely Alex was at school?"

"Well, *sometimes*. To be honest Paul didn't really believe in sending Alex to school. Thought it was more useful for him to get a practical education on the canal. Anyway, here he is." Janice smiled warmly at Alex as he returned from the bathroom. "Budge up, Elspeth," she said. "Alex wants to sit down."

"Oh no, I don't. Really, I'm fine here," said Alex, standing awkwardly and looking desperately for an escape route.

"Don't be silly. Go on, Elspeth. You go to the end and Alex can sit in the middle."

Elspeth moved along to the edge of the sofa, which left *just* enough space for Alex to squeeze in between the two women. Elspeth's hips and legs were touching his. She suddenly felt very hot again.

"Funny that you two should meet each other," Janice continued. "I was just telling Elspeth about how I knew Paul. I've always thought of myself as a bit of a mother figure to you, Alex. When you think about it, you and Elspeth are almost like brother and sister."

Alex made a spluttering noise and somehow spilt his tea-cup of Chardonnay over his jeans. "I don't think ... well, biologically, clearly we're not ... I mean, that would just be ... No."

"Let me get you a cloth for that," said Elspeth, nodding to the wet patch on Alex's lap and grateful for an excuse to exit the strange dynamic on the sofa. "And some more wine."

"I'll come with you," said Alex desperately, clearly now ready for a break from Janice, his apparently honorary mother.

Elspeth and Alex squeezed back into the kitchen. Minnie had disappeared, presumably into one of the other tiny spaces on the boat, and Ava gratefully sat down for a rest on the sofa next to Janice where they were immediately joined by Rick, the conversation with Stephen on drill bits clearly having drawn to a natural close. Elspeth and Alex were alone in the kitchen – well, as alone as they could be on a forty-five foot narrow boat with seven other people on board.

"I had no idea that you knew Janice," began Elspeth. "*Or* that you were close to Reggie. It must have been a bit strange for you, a girl you had never even met suddenly coming and living on *The Blue Belle*." Elspeth paused. "I'm sorry if I was a bit insensitive or ... I don't know. I just hadn't really joined the dots and realised that Reggie would have been part of a community. Did you know Reggie well?"

Alex nodded. "Pretty well," he said. "After my dad, Paul, died a few years ago, Reggie looked out for me, you know? Reggie was a bit of a tricky customer at times – not really one to compromise, as you've probably gathered – but he was a genuinely good person. A loyal person. He really loved your mother." He nodded at Janice. "But he said they could never have made it work as a relationship. I get the impression she's not really one for compromise either," said Alex mischievously.

"*That's* an understatement," agreed Elspeth. "She's a nightmare. And what was all that about her being like a mother to you? I'm guessing she was overexaggerating somewhat."

"Yes. Definitely. But I can *sort of* understand what she means. I never knew my mother; she left my dad a few months after I was born. He never really talked about it so I don't know what the circumstances were. I sometimes wonder whether maybe she just didn't want *me* ... anyway, I didn't really have a female figure in my life while I was growing up. Just dad and Reggie. So when Reggie started seeing Janice, I suppose she did mother me a tiny bit. But I *definitely* couldn't see you in a sisterly way," he finished, blushing slightly.

Elspeth felt her embarrassment coming to the fore. Of course, Alex wouldn't want to be associated with her after the way she had behaved towards him when they first met. "Well, no, obviously not. I mean, it's not as if we've got off to a very good start with each other, is it? You must think I'm so rude after the way I spoke to you on the first day we met. I'm sorry about that," she continued when she saw

Alex was about to interrupt. "I understand now that I did need to move *The Blue Belle*; I just didn't realise it at the time. And, to be honest, I was just a bit overwhelmed by the storm and by ... well, everything that was going on at the time. I just wanted to hide and to batten down the hatches, so to speak, so when you came and told me to move ..."

"You don't need to apologise," said Alex. "I went about things in completely the wrong way. It was me who was rude, not you. I'm sorry."

Elspeth met Alex's gaze and gave him a conciliatory smile.

"And when I said I couldn't see you in a sisterly way," Alex continued, his blush deepening even further, "I didn't mean it was because I don't like you. If anything it's because I –"

To Elspeth's frustration, a rather agitated Nina grabbed her arm before Alex could finish his sentence.

"Elspeth! I need to talk to you. Urgently," said Nina, clearly more than a little tipsy now.

"Can you just give me a few minutes, Nina?" asked Elspeth, looking meaningfully at Alex.

"No! I need to know now! Come to the toilet with me," Nina demanded.

Alex looked a little alarmed. "I don't think she means literally," muttered Elspeth as Nina steered her away from the kitchen. "I'll be back soon."

"So what's so important?" asked Elspeth, once she and Nina were ensconced in the tiny shower room with the door shut behind them.

"We need to talk about Henry," said Nina.

"We do? What is there to talk about?" asked Elspeth.

Nina took a deep breath. "Look, Elspeth, I know we haven't been friends for very long, and this is *exactly* the kind of thing that breaks up a friendship, but I have to ask: are things serious with you and Henry?"

"No!" exclaimed Elspeth, realising in that moment that she'd actually *forgotten* that her and Henry might even be a thing. "We've only been on one date! Henry's nice and everything, but the chemistry just isn't there. Why are you – *Oh*!" The penny dropped as Elspeth remembered walking into the shower room earlier to find Nina and Henry hiding in there, deep in conversation. Come to think of it, Henry had spent most of the evening so far with Nina. She would never have predicted it, but there was only one logical conclusion. "Nina do *you* like Henry?" she asked.

"Yes! I *really* like him!" exclaimed Nina. "He's perfect! He's so intelligent and thoughtful, but absolutely *not* an alpha male, you know? I can't stand alpha males. Well, I guess maybe I'm a bit of an alpha myself, so it just doesn't work. But obviously if he's with you, then I wouldn't – "

"No, he's definitely *not* with me. I mean, we haven't had a conversation about it one way or the other, but as far as I'm concerned Henry is available."

"Can I tell him you said that? Because I think he isn't sure how things stand. And he's so honourable that he wouldn't want to do anything inappropriate. Even though," Nina leaned in conspiratorially, despite the fact that they were the only ones in the tiny shower room, "I'm pretty sure that he'd like something to happen between us tonight!"

"That's great, Nina," said Elspeth sincerely. She was genuinely happy for her, and for Henry as well if the feeling was mutual. She was also desperate to return to her conversation with Alex.

"So, Nina, if that's all you needed, then yay! Go for it!" Elspeth nudged a flushed and excited Nina out of the shower room and gently guided her in Henry's direction before returning to the galley kitchen, where Alex was still standing, carefully pouring some of the 'White Wine' into his floral teacup.

"Alex! Sorry about that. Glad to see you're helping yourself. Is all the Chablis all gone?"

"Looks like it," said Alex. "This one was open, so I thought I'd try it." He took a sip and made a face. "Wow. Tangy. Is that *definitely* wine?"

"Supposedly," said Elspeth. "Anyway, sorry we got interrupted. You were just saying that you couldn't see me in a sisterly way because ..."

"Yes, well," Alex blushed a little and he looked intently at his tea cup of White Wine. "It's just that ever since I saw you, that first day on *The Blue Belle*, I've had this feeling that -"

"Elspeth! I need to talk to you!" A flushed Minnie staggered into the galley kitchen and grabbed Elspeth's arm.

"Can it wait a minute, Minnie? I'm just in the middle of something."

"No, you're not, you're just chatting in the kitchen. *He* won't mind. It's important! Come to the toilet with me."

"Really?" interjected Alex. "Another one?"

Elspeth gritted her teeth. "I *really will* be back in a minute," she said to Alex. "Just ... hold that thought."

Elspeth found herself back in the tiny shower room of the narrow boat.

"This *really* isn't a good time, Minnie! What's so important?"

"I need to talk to you about Stephen," said Minnie earnestly, sitting down on the closed toilet seat.

"Stephen? What about him? *Oh*!" Here we go again, thought Elspeth. It was a good job she *wasn't* actually interested in either of the men she had been seeing. Her friends were unstoppable. "Let me guess. You like Stephen, and you think that he likes you, but you're not sure whether I have feelings for him so you're doing the honourable thing and checking first. Correct?"

"Yes. How did you –"

"Just a hunch. Yes. Fine with me. In fact, it would be great if you *could* date him, because he's excellent with engines and electrics, so I could do with staying in contact with him for the odd favour. Right, can I leave the bathroom now?"

"Thank you, Elspeth! You're amazing! I *told* Stephen you wouldn't mind ..." Minnie muttered as they left the bathroom. "Stephen! She said it's fine!" she yelled across *The Blue Belle* before making a bee line for him.

Elspeth calculated that there shouldn't be any more interruptions. Janice and Rick were already a couple and Ava was quite settled with Matt, so Elspeth didn't imagine anyone else would need her permission for their romantic entanglements. She could go back to her conversation with Alex and he might *actually* be able to finish his sentence; Elspeth was desperate to hear whatever it was he wanted to say.

Slipping back into the galley kitchen, Elspeth couldn't see Alex anywhere. She looked up and down the length of the boat – he wasn't in the saloon either. She squeezed past her guests to pop her head behind the curtain in the bedroom, only to see Stephen and

Minnie locked in an embrace. She quickly retreated, pulling the curtain behind her. Seeing Janice and Rick still seated snugly on the sofa, she approached them. "Have either of you seen Alex?" she asked.

"He's just left, love," said Rick helpfully. "A few minutes ago."

Elspeth's heart sank. "Oh! It's just ... we were in the middle of a conversation, that's all. Did he say why he was going?"

Rick shook his head. "Nope. He was having a chat with those other two men – Stephen and the solicitor one – then he left."

Elspeth felt the blood rush to her face. Alex talking with Stephen and Henry ... Now *that* wasn't a good mix.

"Thanks Rick," she muttered, before turning to see Henry and Nina fully immersed in conversation by the wood-burner. She needed to know what Henry and Stephen had said to Alex; she went over to them. "Henry! Hi!"

"Elspeth? I hope this isn't awkward? Me and Nina just hit it off and I wasn't sure if me and you were a thing but she said we're not?"

"No, we're not," Elspeth reassured him. "That's all fine, Henry. I think we're better just as friends. But there's a reason I came over ... When I was in the bathroom just now, you were talking to Alex and Stephen. What were you all talking about?"

Henry blushed. "Well, actually, we were talking about you? Not in a bad way, of course. Alex was just asking me and Stephen how we knew you? And so I said that we'd been on a couple of dates but I wasn't sure where it was going? And then Stephen said about the ... you know ... the evening with him? And the kiss? Which I was a bit surprised about, but anyway ... and then Alex said he was leaving?"

Elspeth felt a bit faint. What kind impression would Alex have of her now? Obviously, she *had* been on a couple of dates with Henry and she *had* had a spontaneous kiss with Stephen, but there hadn't been anything deliberately deceptive. She knew, though, that it didn't exactly cast her in a positive light.

"I didn't say anything wrong, did I?" asked Henry anxiously. "I didn't think it was a secret or anything?"

"No," Elspeth reassured him. "You didn't say anything wrong, Henry. I just ... perhaps I need to clarify things a little with Alex, that's all. I'll leave you to it."

Elspeth went outside to the prow of the boat for a little fresh air. Her boat warming, it seemed, had been a roaring success. Everyone had enjoyed themselves and had left the evening happily partnered up; except for her. And Alex.

Chapter 20: Explanations

It was past midnight by the time Elspeth's guests left *The Blue Belle*, and Elspeth exhaustedly assessed the detritus left by the barge-warming. She knew it would take her most of the morning to clear up the bottles and crisp packets and do all of the washing up. As she got into her pyjamas, she reflected that she didn't exactly have anything *else* to do until her lunchtime shift at *The Waterside*: her friends were all now happily coupled up and the man *she* was interested in presumably thought she was some sort of manipulative man-eater. With the work on *The Blue Belle* finished, Elspeth would need to find something else to focus her time on.

The next morning, her head slightly fuzzy after the late night and the alcohol, Elspeth set about clearing up after her guests. It took her a couple of hours to get *The Blue Belle* shiny and orderly. She was just surveying the space with some satisfaction and wondering whether to relax with a book on her sofa until her shift at the café started, when there was a knock at the door. Elspeth opened it with trepidation. She felt instinctively that it would be one of her guests from the previous evening, but had no idea which one.

Janice. Elspeth groaned inwardly. She had something of a hangover, she had spent the last two hours cleaning, and she felt rather disheartened at the events of last night and the impression Alex must now have of her. The last thing she wanted was an interaction with her uncompromising and critical mother.

"Hi mum," said Elspeth warily. "I *definitely* didn't send you a message inviting you over this time – what are you doing here?"

"Just thought we should have a little chat," said Janice, barging past Elspeth onto *The Blue Belle* and making straight for the sofa. "Are you going to make me a cup of tea or not?"

Wordlessly and somewhat resentfully, Elspeth put the kettle on and popped two tea bags into a pair of pastel blue mugs adorned with pretty daisies. Taking Janice her tea, she sat next to her on the sofa and waited for her to explain the reason for her visit. For once, she was intrigued rather than irritated when Janice spoke.

"I thought we should talk about Alex," said Janice bluntly.

Elspeth couldn't hide her surprise. "Alex?"

Janice nodded. "Now, I know that you're *technically* my daughter, but Alex is like a son to me. I don't want to see him getting hurt."

"*Technically* your daughter? Thanks mum, that means a lot. And what do you mean, you don't want to see Alex getting hurt? What's that got to do with me?"

Janice rolled her eyes. "You really can be a bit dim sometimes Elspeth," she said. "It's obvious to anybody that Alex likes you. Sexually, I mean."

Elspeth blushed and stared intently at her mug of tea. She *really* would rather Janice refrained from using words like that; it was very discomfiting in a mother. "I mean, I suppose you are *quite* attractive," Janice continued obliviously, "despite having your father's nose. Anyway, that's obviously why Alex came last night. Quite a big thing for him to put himself out there like that, what with everything he's been through. I think you should know what you're dealing with before you mess him about even more."

"Mess him about *even more*? I'm not messing anyone about! But," Elspeth's curiosity got the better of her, "what do you mean, what he's been through?"

"Well, I'm not sure where to start really," said Janice. "A biscuit or two might help me to focus, if it wouldn't be too much trouble to offer a little refreshment to your own mother, Elspeth."

With a resigned sigh, Elspeth raided her biscuit tin and came up with a few bourbons. "Right. There. You were saying?"

Janice kept her waiting a few moments while she slowly dunked her bourbon in her tea, then continued with the air of a wise story-teller. "Well, I suppose you should know about what happened with his mum first."

Elspeth nodded. "He said something about it last night. Didn't she leave when he was a baby?"

Janice nodded. "Interesting that he told you," she commented. "He doesn't usually talk about it at all. But yes, she left a few months after he was born. Obviously it wasn't a planned pregnancy – well, I know what *that's* like – but the way she left Paul like that with Alex as a baby was very difficult for Paul. Not so much as a letter or a visit since. Alex doesn't know his mother at all."

Elspeth was momentarily speechless. She wasn't sure which of Janice's comments to address first. "Hang on a minute, mum. What do you mean, *I know what that's like*? Was *I* not planned?"

"Of course not!" said Janice through a mouthful of bourbon. "I always assumed you knew that. I was a vibrant young woman with opportunities, and I wasn't sure that I wanted to commit to your *father*. But, well, it happened. And I stayed with your father, for a few years at least, so that we could bring you up together."

Now that Janice said it, Elspeth realised it wasn't *that* much of a surprise; if she had considered it deeply, she would probably have drawn the conclusion herself. Still, it didn't make it any easier to hear, and Janice's method of frank, offhand delivery wasn't exactly sensitive. Elspeth decided that it was something she would ruminate on privately and perhaps raise with Janice another time; for now, she wanted to hear what Janice had to say about Alex.

"So, Alex's mother. Did Alex's father – Paul, I think you said - did *he* know why she left?"

Janice shrugged. "Sort of. He knew she didn't want to be a mother, and I don't think things were all that rosy between her and Paul anyway. There might've been somebody else involved too; Paul always suspected that but he never knew for sure. The hardest bit for him was the way she did it, though. Just took off in the middle of the night while Paul and Alex were asleep. No note, no explanation, no discussion. So there was Paul, only in his twenties, the sole carer for a little baby on a canal boat." Janice sipped her tea. "I didn't know him at that time, of course. It was a few years later that I met Reggie and got to know Paul and Alex. But he talked to me about it a fair bit. I was like a sister to him, really."

Elspeth rolled her eyes. Janice's imaginary non-biological family seemed to grow by the minute.

"And what about Alex?" asked Elspeth. "What effect did all of this have on him?"

"Well, he was happy enough as a little boy, I suppose. He didn't really know any different. Just him and Paul, living on *The Briar Rose* together and messing around by the canal all day. Not a bad life for a little'un. No, the problems started when Alex was old enough for school. Paul didn't believe in schooling, you see. He hadn't had much education when he was growing up, and he didn't see why it should be different for Alex. So he didn't send him. Caused all sorts of problems. They'd have the truant officers around at the boat, threatening to take Paul to court over it all, and the funny thing was, Alex actually *wanted* to go to school! I think he started to resent Paul as he got older; saw him as standing in his way, making him feel different to other kids. So Alex tried to educate himself a bit: always had his nose in a book, reading goodness' knows what. But he never got what you'd call a proper education. He sat those exams – the same ones you did – the GCSEs? But he only got a couple. Not enough to do anything with. I suppose that's why he works on the canals now – it's the only thing he knows."

Elspeth nodded. She imagined the young Alex, longingly watching his peers go off to school in their smart uniforms while he stayed on the boat with Paul. She could understand why he had wanted to join them. She found herself feeling unusually thankful that Janice was her mother: whatever her eccentricities, she had always been there for Elspeth, in her own particular way, and had never prevented her from accessing opportunities or spending time with her peers.

"And did Paul and Alex ever hear from his mother?" asked Elspeth.

Janice shook her head. "Nope. When he was in his teens, Alex tried to find her. Persuaded Paul to go cruising on *The Briar Rose* for a few months to see if they could track her down. She's probably living on the water somewhere now – if she's still alive, that is. That was all she'd ever known, too. But they couldn't find her. I don't think Alex has ever let go of the idea, to be honest. You're lucky, Elspeth, having a dedicated mother like me. Sacrificed myself for you, you know."

For once, Elspeth didn't feel the urge to argue. "And what about Alex now?" she asked. "I mean, you said Paul passed away a few years' ago. Is Alex just ... on his own now?"

Janice nodded. "*Now* he is. But for a long time he wasn't. She was bad news, that one," she said mysteriously.

"Which one?"

"Katie. Alex's ex. He was with her for, oh, at least five years. Difficult woman, if you ask me."

Well, you should know, thought Elspeth. "Difficult in what way? And what happened between them?"

"Well, she was attractive alright – I have to give her that. It was like she cast a spell on poor Alex. But oh, she was manipulative. He couldn't do anything without her say so. She moved in with him on *The Briar Rose* – a bit of a freeloader, in my opinion – and he wasn't even allowed off the boat without explaining himself. Whereas her? *She* was out at all hours, seeing whomever she pleased. Anyway, she knew all about Alex's past; his mother abandoning him; leaving in the middle of the night without a word. And do you know what she did?"

Elspeth waited, eyes wide, for Janice to explain.

"She did *exactly the same thing*. Left *The Briar Rose* in the middle of the night. No note, no explanation, no discussion. It was as if she did it deliberately to hurt him. Katie knew how he felt about what had happened with his mother; all of those unanswered questions, wondering for all those years whether it was his fault that she'd left. And then he has to go through it again with *her*; bringing up all those old memories, all those insecurities. Well, you can imagine," Janice concluded, "Alex has a few issues when it comes to trusting women. And then you go and mess him about like that. Honestly, Elspeth. You can be very insensitive sometimes."

Elspeth opened her mouth to protest, then closed it again. She knew from experience that there was no point in trying to reason with Janice. Besides, she realised as she glanced at the pretty clock on the wall of the galley kitchen, she was due at *The Waterside* in fifteen minutes. Bidding Janice goodbye and ushering her off *The Blue Belle*, Elspeth reflected on their conversation as she picked up her bag and headed to the café for her afternoon shift. Three things had become clear to her during the events of the last twenty-four hours. Firstly, and most startlingly, she knew beyond a doubt that there was *something* between her and Alex. She was certainly attracted to him, and the fact that Janice had decided to warn her not to mess around with Alex's feelings suggested that Alex's behaviour indicated that he was attracted to her too. Secondly, she understood that Alex clearly had reasons to be wary around women; he had been hurt in the past and, if ever there might be a chance of anything happening between them, Elspeth would need to be sensitive to this. Thirdly, and most frustratingly, Elspeth realised that the events of the previous evening had probably *put paid* to any chance of something happening between them. Alex had come to her barge-warming with a nice bottle of wine as requested, and had tried, Elspeth was now convinced, to tell her in the kitchen that he felt a connection between them. He had been rudely interrupted, twice, then had been informed by Henry and Stephen that they were *both* seeing Elspeth in one form or another. Given Alex's past, any

183

suggestion that Elspeth was untrustworthy would be the ultimate red flag. Oh dear.

Elspeth felt she might understand a little of what Alex had experienced. She had never *really* known her father; not properly, at any rate. He and Janice had got divorced when Elspeth was around ten years old. Until that point, he had been around when he wasn't working at his office job, and Elspeth had formed a vague impression of him as a weary, somewhat defeated figure. He had clearly always been terrified of Janice. When Janice had dramatically announced one day that she was divorcing him as he was a "pathetic excuse for a man", he had seemed to be somewhat relieved to have managed to escape without needing to confront her directly, and had sloped off without complaint to a one-bedroom flat in Milton Keynes. Elspeth would usually receive a card and an often misguided gift from him on her birthday and at Christmas time, but she rarely saw him. As a child, it didn't occur to her to question the relationship: Janice never alluded to him and Elspeth accepted the situation as it was presented to her. It was only as an adult that Elspeth had attempted to build a relationship of sorts. By this time, though, her father was more distant than ever. He was polite enough when she called and he agreed to meet her on occasion, but he clearly had no emotional space for her in his solitary life. When he had passed away four years ago, Elspeth had felt sadness at the fact that she had never been able to connect with him and that, uncomfortable though it was to face, he hadn't really wanted a relationship with her. It wasn't the same as Alex's mother's abandonment of him, she knew, but she understood something of what it was like to feel unloved by a parent.

Sundays were often one of the busier days at *The Waterside*, what with day trippers coming to spend a few hours by the canal-side, and Elspeth knew that there would be a steady stream of customers to distract her from her disappointment. Anna was busy in the kitchen grilling bacon and buttering bread rolls when she arrived.

"Rough night, Elspeth?" she asked.

"Oh no, do I look that bad?"

"Well, *you* can carry it off, but you're not exactly your usual bright self!" grinned Anna.

Elspeth gave a wry smile and put on the apron she always wore for work. She quickly fell into the rhythm of taking orders, clearing tables and serving food, feeling slightly numb as she went through the motions. She was surprised to hear a friendly little bark behind her, and couldn't help but brighten as Daphne came trotting towards her. Instinctively, Elspeth stooped down to greet the little dog with open arms, before processing what Daphne's presence would mean. Alex. She looked up, half desperate to see him and half dreading an interaction with him. There he was, wearing a mid-blue t-shirt and dark blue jeans with brown boots. He looked like he'd just stepped out of some sort of outdoor activities commercial.

Elspeth took a deep breath. "Alex. Hi. It's good to see you. About last night. I – well, I think you might have got slightly the wrong impression of me. I'm glad you're here; I'd like it if we could clear things up a bit."

Alex raised his eyebrows. "Yes. I think I *did* get the wrong impression of you," he said slowly. "When you invited me to your barge-warming, I thought maybe it was because you liked me. Or something. I don't know." He paused. "Why *did* you invite me, Elspeth?"

"Oh! Well, I didn't, really."

"You definitely did. You messaged me."

"Yes. I know *that*. But I didn't *mean* to message you." Elspeth felt relieved to have the chance to explain the mix up. "You see, I've got this new phone and I'm not really used to using it, so I only invited you by mistake ..."

Alex looked mortified. "So you mean to tell me that I turned up with a bottle of wine and a packet of kettle chips to a party that I *wasn't invited to*?"

"Well, yes, but –"

"Why didn't you tell me? Do you feel *sorry* for me or something? I have got other things to do with my Saturday night, you know."

'Yes, well, I'm sure you have. But, you see, when you turned up, I realised that actually I would quite like to have you there, because ... well, because - "

"Because you like to have a few men around who you can string along? Is two not enough?"

"No!" Now Elspeth was mortified. Was that really what he thought of her? "Look, I know the situation with Henry and Stephen looks a bit ... inappropriate ... but really, there isn't anything going on with either of them now. I've only been on two dates with Henry, and one of *them* was unintentional, and I just kissed Stephen once on the spur of the moment! I'm not *with* either of them. And besides, I didn't mean to invite *them* to the barge-warming, either!"

Alex looked at Elspeth incredulously. "You really do need to learn some basic social rules," he muttered. "Like how to not unintentionally go on dates and inadvertently invite people to parties."

Elspeth was lost for words for a moment as she reflected on the utter ridiculousness of the events of the previous evening, then, against her better judgement, she started to laugh. Alex froze for a moment, clearly unsure how to respond. Elspeth met his gaze, her eyes full of warmth and humour, and she saw Alex visibly relax. To her utter relief and delight, he started to laugh too.

Chapter 21: Possibility

"I'm so sorry. About all of it. You must think I'm completely socially inept," said Elspeth, as her and Alex sat at one of the outdoor tables at *The Waterside*. Anna had seen Elspeth talking with Alex and given her a nod to suggest they sit down. Somehow everyone else could see that there was something between them, and also that they needed a few nudges in the right direction so that they didn't manage to mess it up again.

Alex grinned. "Your behaviour has been a bit ... unusual," he said mischievously. "I can honestly say that I don't know anyone else quite like you."

Anna came over to their table with two steaming mugs of tea and two full breakfasts. "On the house," she said with a smile. "I think this one might be feeling a bit delicate today," she nodded to Elspeth. "Apparently she had something of an eventful evening."

"It was eventful alright," agreed Alex. "Thank you."

Anna nodded and left them to it. "So, there's a few things I don't understand," said Alex. "Actually, more than a few."

"Where do you want to start?" asked Elspeth.

Alex took a deep breath. "Maybe from the beginning?"

Elspeth nodded.

"So, I guess you don't remember me from when we were children, do you?" he said shyly.

"No, I don't – " began Elspeth, but suddenly another memory washed over her. Trying to squeeze herself behind an old cupboard on *The Blue Belle* while she played hide and seek. Of course, she hadn't been playing hide and seek on her own! There had been another child there. A little boy, with big green eyes and unruly dark hair. She could picture him now, even down to the too-small Teenage Mutant Ninja Turtles tracksuit he had been wearing. She remembered Reggie's letter: *You and that boy playing hide and seek in the saloon.* Of course she remembered Alex. *Of course* she did!

Elspeth looked at Alex with wide eyes. "Teenage Mutant Ninja Turtles!" she exclaimed.

Now it was Alex's turn to look confused. "Um ..."

"Your tracksuit! I remember it! It was too small for you – I thought you must be really tall because the trousers only came half way down your legs!"

Alex burst out laughing again. "You remember *that*? Wow. I'd forgotten about that tracksuit. I loved it at the time. Goodness knows why – it was hideous!"

Elspeth nodded vehemently. "It really was. But listen, I *do* remember you. I just ... it's weird ... I hadn't accessed that memory for a long time. My childhood memories are like that. Sometimes I just get a kind of snapshot of something. I'd certainly never made the connection with you. I mean, you've grown quite a bit since then." Elspeth found herself blushing inexplicably.

Alex nodded. "I get that. It's just ... oh, it's silly. Never mind."

"No, go on."

"Well, much as I don't like to admit it, I didn't have any friends when I was a child. Dad didn't send me to school most of the time and so, whenever I did go, I was on the outside of all of the little friendship groups, you know? Plus I was always known as the weird kid who lived on a barge and kept truanting. Not that I wanted to truant," Alex added earnestly. "I

189

think I was the only kid in my class who actually *wanted* to go to school. Anyway, I didn't have any friends, much less anyone to play with outside of school. No playdates, nothing like that. So when you came to visit Reggie on *The Blue Belle* with Janice, and me and Dad came over, it was ..." Now it was Alex's turn to blush deeply. "It was the closest thing I had experienced to having a friend."

Elspeth's heart went out to him. "So it meant a lot to you," she said gently.

Alex nodded. "I think I only saw you three times," he said, "but in my mind, we were friends. I didn't really understand why you stopped coming. I thought, maybe, it was something I had done." He shook his head. "It's silly, isn't it, the way we process things as children?"

Elspeth shook her head. "I can see why you might have thought that," she ventured. "Especially after what happened with your mum."

Alex looked at her questioningly. "Janice came to see me this morning," Elspeth explained. "She didn't tell me *too* much, but I understand a little bit, I think. And just for the record, in case your childhood self is still interested, it certainly wasn't because of anything *you* did that I stopped visiting! I just had to come along with Janice when she told me to. I guess maybe things cooled off with her and Reggie for a while, or maybe there weren't any more teacher training days on a Monday! But then," Elspeth continued to put things together, "when I arrived on *The Blue Belle* as an adult, did you know it was me straight away?"

"I guessed it must be," said Alex. "And you still look the same. The long blonde hair, the big blue eyes, the cute nose."

The cute nose? Elspeth could have married Alex right there and then.

"So why were you so ... well, I don't know how else to say it ... *aggressive* that first time I saw you? That morning of the storm when you were shouting at me from the towpath?"

"Aggressive? Oh, no! Was that how it came across?" Alex looked down at the table. "I'm sorry. I've been told I can come across like that sometimes. I don't mean to. No, I came over that morning because I realised that your Waterside Mooring permit was about to run out. Reggie always renewed his exactly a month before me. Anyway, I saw a note on my calendar the night before to renew mine in advance, and realised that you might not know about it and it was expiring the next day! You can be fined pretty heavily if you overstay. So I wanted to warn you about it. I thought if you just moved to a regular mooring while you sorted it out then you'd avoid the fine. But the weather was awful, and I couldn't hear what you were saying, and you couldn't hear me and ... well, then when you said you didn't know how to move the boat I *was* pretty horrified. I mean, that could be dangerous. But you wouldn't come out and talk to me and I didn't feel like I could come onto the boat without you inviting me to, so ..."

So he had been trying to help her. Of course. "Anyway," Alex continued brightly. "You don't need to worry about it for another six months now, so that should give you plenty of time to decide what you want to do."

Elspeth nodded, then froze with a forkful of beans halfway to her mouth. How did Alex know the mooring had been renewed for a six month period? Elspeth understood that six months was somewhat unusual; a year would be far more standard. The beans dripped slowly from her fork as she concluded the obvious. "It was *you* who renewed the lease for me, wasn't it?" she said slowly.

191

Alex looked a little uncomfortable. "Yes. Well, I didn't know what else to do, really. I didn't want you to get fined and," he suddenly became incredibly interested in his own forkful of beans, "I suppose I didn't want you to leave."

Elspeth was stunned; firstly by the fact that this man who she had insulted had spent hundreds of pounds on her behalf and not even *told* her, and secondly by the fact that, for whatever reason, he wanted her to *stay*. Something swelled in her chest; she looked at Alex until he reluctantly took his gaze away from his baked beans and met hers. "Thank you," she said, giving the words as much weight as she could. "Thank you for helping me. And thank you for wanting me to stay."

Finishing their food and drinks, Elspeth invited Alex to come back to *The Blue Belle* with her; things had been so busy and confusing on the previous evening that he hadn't really seen the completed renovation *properly*, and Elspeth figured this was a good excuse to prolong their meeting. With Daphne running along beside them, seemingly delighted that her two favourite humans had finally decided to take her for a walk *together*, Alex and Elspeth made their way back along the towpath.

"I'd like to explain about Henry and Stephen too," said Elspeth as they walked.

Alex looked uncomfortable. "You don't need to explain," he muttered. "It's really none of my business."

Elspeth fought the urge to tell him then and there that she absolutely *wanted* it to be his business, but decided that the time wasn't quite right. Yet.

"Well, perhaps not, but I'd like the chance to put the record straight," she continued. Elspeth found herself telling Alex a little about her break up with

Peter Penguin and her subsequent decision to keep an open mind about dating. "Then I happened to see Henry one night at one of the pubs along the canal," she explained. Elspeth related Henry's unfortunate drink spillage and his subsequent rather public dumping.

"Ouch. Poor Henry," sympathised Alex.

'Exactly. Anyway, so I went over to sit with him and we had a nice evening together, so when he suggested a second date I thought, *why not*? I mean, it's not as if there were fireworks or anything, but I decided that I might as well give things a chance. So we just ... had another nice drink together one evening and left things open."

Alex nodded. "And Stephen?"

"Well," Elspeth blushed a little at that one. "He came over to have a look at the electrics on *The Blue Belle* for me a few weeks ago and we just hit it off. I mean, he's very easy company, very confident, very open. Then as he was leaving he said he was going to have dinner at the pub and asked if I'd like to join him. It wasn't planned or anything. So we had a fun evening and, when he walked me home, we had a ... moment. But then he came to do the electrics the following week and barely mentioned it! I get the impression that Stephen's just a spontaneous kind of person. So there wasn't really anything much happening romantically with either of them," Elspeth continued. "Which is a good job, considering they've been poached by Minnie and Nina!"

Alex smiled. "Yes, your friends are certainly ... assertive. And, you know, maybe that's a good thing," he added shyly. "Because presumably that means that you are well and truly, definitely, irrefutably single."

"And that's a *good* thing?" returned Elspeth playfully.

"*I* think so," said Alex softly. They had by now reached *The Blue Belle*, and Elspeth took out her key to let them into the calm, intimate space. She felt a warm glow spreading over her at Alex's words.

"You really have done an amazing job in here, Elspeth," said Alex, as they surveyed her new home. "It's almost unrecognisable compared to when Reggie had it. He'd be proud of what you've achieved, Elspeth. I'm sure of it."

"Thank you," she murmured, as she and Alex sat down side by side on the squishy sofa. "So, just now, when you said you thought it was a good thing I'm single now, what *exactly* did you mean?"

"This," said Alex, leaning in to kiss her. Elspeth responded immediately; she couldn't quite believe that this was happening. She wanted to stay here, on this sofa, in this embrace, forever.

"Elspeth! Elspeth! Are you in there? It's your mother!"

"Oh no, not *now*," Elspeth muttered through gritted teeth as she pulled away ever so slightly from Alex. "That woman really *does* pick her moments."

"Maybe she'll go away," Alex whispered into Elspeth's hair.

Elspeth tilted her face up to look up at him. "You know Janice, right?"

"Fair point. She'll be peeping through that window any moment ... now!"

Sure enough, as Alex spoke, Janice's nylon-clad legs appeared at the window and they heard her berating Rick.

"*You'll* need to get down there to have a look. I can't bend that far. She's probably fallen asleep on the sofa with a hangover." Janice rudely tapped on the window with the toe of her shoe. "Elspeth!

Elspeth! You seemed a bit miserable this morning. Me and Rick have come to cheer you up!"

"Is she in there?" This time it was a *somewhat* more welcome voice: Minnie. "Hi Janice! Me and Stephen wanted to come over to check Elspeth's alright after last night. It was all a bit, you know, *awkward*, what with me and Stephen getting together. Oh, hi, Nina!"

Elspeth groaned and looked desperately at Alex. "I don't think we have any choice," he said.

"You're right," agreed Elspeth. "Let's just start the motor and sail off now."

Alex grinned. "I think we need to face them first," he said. "But I like your thinking, Elspeth Henley."

Smoothing down her hair after approximately four minutes of alone time with Alex, Elspeth reluctantly made her way to the door of *The Blue Belle*, to see Janice, Rick, Minnie, Stephen, Nina and Henry assembled like some sort of awkward, ill-advised welcoming party. "Elspeth! We all had the same idea after last night," said Minnie helpfully. "We were a bit worried about you after ... you know. So we've come to cheer you up! I've just messaged Ava; she's on her way with Matt. Oh!" Minnie was somewhat thrown to see Alex emerge from the doorway behind Elspeth. "Oh, I see! We didn't know you had company already. We'll, um ... leave you to it."

"It's fine, Minnie," said Elspeth generously, looking back at Alex to check he was on board with her approach. "Seeing as you're all here anyway, why don't we go and grab a drink?"

"I thought you'd never ask," grumbled Janice. "Come on, Rick. Let's get going to the pub. Ava and her bloke can meet us there."

Snuggled in a corner booth at *The Duck Inn*, surrounded by her friends and family, Alex's hand holding hers firmly under the table, Elspeth was overcome by a sense of immense gratitude at the turn her life had taken over the last few months. She had *thought* that she was previously on the right path; with Peter, with her job, with her flat, but now she realised that, while that might be the perfect life for someone, it would never have been the perfect life for her. In bequeathing *The Blue Belle* to her, Reggie had opened up a whole new landscape for Elspeth: a new home, a new job, and most importantly, exciting new people in her life. She glanced shyly at Alex, only to see that he was already looking at her. She wasn't usually a one for big speeches, but Elspeth felt a sudden urge to say something. Clearing her throat to get everyone's attention, she raised her glass. "I'd like to raise a toast to the man who made all of this possible," she said humbly. "To Reggie."

"To Reggie." The voices echoed around the table.

"And to *The Blue Belle*," offered Janice, with uncharacteristic good timing and good humour.

"To *The Blue Belle*!" As her friends and family raised their glasses to her new home, Elspeth couldn't help but feel there would be many more adventures to come.

A couple of drinks later, the little party began to break up: Minnie and Stephen were clearly keen to get back to Minnie's flat for a bit of alone time, and Nina and Henry both wanted to get a bit of rest before starting their demanding work weeks. As for Janice, she seemed surprisingly pleased with Elspeth for a change, and took her to one side for a moment. "He's a good one, that one," she said, nodding at Alex. "I could never really make it work with a man;

not properly. But you're different to me, Elspeth. Now go and christen that new barge of yours."

Elspeth wasn't entirely convinced by Janice's rather forward approach, but for once she appreciated Janice's sentiment. As her friends and family dispersed, Elspeth found herself alone outside the pub with Alex, whose eyes had barely left her face for the previous couple of hours. "So, I believe we were rather rudely interrupted earlier," said Elspeth. "How about we go back to *The Blue Belle* and finish our ... conversation?"

Alex nodded. "There is literally nothing I would rather do," he said warmly, falling into step beside her as they made their way back along on the towpath, hand in hand. As they let themselves into *The Blue Belle*, Elspeth kept hold of Alex's hand and led him to the back of the boat. "I'm not sure that you got to see the bedroom yesterday," she said mischievously, drawing back the curtain to reveal the freshly decorated space, painted in a romantic pale blue in order to differentiate it from the main, sage-green living area of the boat.

"No, I didn't," concurred Alex, glancing admiringly around the small room. "I bet it's really cosy in here when you close that." He nodded to the heavy curtain that Elspeth had erected as a screen.

"It is," Elspeth agreed. She had waited long enough. "I'll show you, if you like." And with that, Elspeth quietly drew the heavy damask curtain. Alone at last.

Coming in 2024 …

Elspeth and "The Blue Belle" – Book Two: Uncertain Waters

Elspeth Henley is delighted with her new life on *The Blue Belle*, the narrow boat unexpectedly bequeathed to her by her mother's ex-lover, Reggie. Having made a home for herself on the British Waterways, Elspeth is excited for the next chapter in her life, not least because she has met someone: the gorgeous and unconventional Alex, himself the owner of a neighbouring boat, *The Briar Rose*.

But despite their desire to focus on their new relationship and to try to build a life together, Elspeth and Alex find that, whether they like it or not, they have other matters – and people – claiming their attention. Alex's past simply won't leave him alone: a problematic letter from his estranged mother and unsettling rumours about his ex-girlfriend lead Alex and Elspeth to embark on their first cruise on *The Blue Belle* in search of the answers that Alex so desperately needs. Not to be outdone, Elspeth's mother Janice decides that she needs a holiday with her beau, Rick, and Elspeth finds that she has her impossible mother along for the ride. Yet, as things turn out, Janice might be just the person they need to help set the record straight.

Will Elspeth and Alex find the answers they are seeking in order to move forward in their lives? And can *The Blue Belle* provide them with the sanctuary that they need?

Also by this author:

The Isabella

Desperate to escape the uninspiring future that awaits her, twenty-one year old Maria agrees to max out her credit card for a holiday on a Greek island with her irrepressible best friend Kat. A chance encounter with the assured, wealthy Antonio leads to an unexpected invitation for the girls to join him and his charming nephew, Eduardo, on their sleek superyacht, 'The Isabella', where Maria finds herself immersed in a world of luxury and opportunity that she could previously have only ever dreamed of.

But when Kat leaves to return home to England, Maria finds that the decadent allure of life on 'The Isabella' masks a dark secret. Unsure of who she can trust, Maria has to rely on her own initiative and cunning to search for the truth. What are Antonio's ulterior motives for keeping Maria on the yacht? What is the role of the unfriendly Rosa? And is Eduardo's growing closeness with Maria all just part of their plan?

Maria must piece together the evidence to save herself. In being deceived, she must become the deceiver.

The Treasures of Hawthorn Cottage

Lilian Farrier is an artist. Yet as an uneducated, unmarried woman living in Victorian England, she doubts that she would ever be taken seriously by the art world. Crafting her masterpieces in the secrecy of her father's tiny attic, her brother Edmund is the only one who knows of her talent. It is when Lilian's circumstances change and she faces the stark reality of going into service that she and Edmund hatch a plan: to sell her paintings in his name.

'The Treasures of Hawthorn Cottage' follows the intertwining stories of Lilian and the three women whose lives are tied to her legacy: Eva, falsely accused of adultery in the 1930s by her philandering husband; Anna, an unmarried mother ostracised by her family in the 1960s; and Katya, an ambitious over-achiever in the 2020s who begins to question the purpose of her corporate success. The tiny, remote Hawthorn Cottage, nestled in the rolling landscape of the Derbyshire Dales, holds treasures for each of them.

The women's four interconnected stories explore their challenges, dreams and triumphs. Each is thwarted by the social expectations imposed upon them, yet each ultimately finds a way to thrive, thanks to the sanctuary of Hawthorn Cottage and to one woman's far-reaching artistic legacy.

Printed in Great Britain
by Amazon